Meet Ann M. Martin

Ann M. Martin is the author of the bestselling
Baby-Sitters Club series, which sold
176 million copies worldwide. In addition, she is
the author of over thirty critically-acclaimed novels,
including *A Corner of the Universe* which won a Newbery
Honor in 2003, and *How to Look for a Lost Dog*, which
was published to widespread praise.

This book is for my nephew, Henry McGrath,
a dog's best friend

First published in the UK in 2016 by Usborne Publishing Ltd., Usborne House,
83-85 Saffron Hill, London EC1N 8RT, England. www.usborne.com

Text © Ann M. Martin, 2005

The right of Ann M. Martin to be identified as the author of this work has been
asserted by her in accordance with the Copyright, Designs and Patents Act, 1988.

Cover illustration by Antonia Miller.

The name Usborne and the devices ♀ 🌐 are Trade Marks of
Usborne Publishing Ltd.

This is a work of fiction. The characters, incidents, and dialogues are products of the
author's imagination and are not to be construed as real. Any resemblance to actual
events or persons, living or dead, is entirely coincidental.

A CIP catalogue record for this book is available from the British Library.

JFMAM JASOND/16 ISBN 9781474926393 04303/1

Printed in the UK.

A DOG'S LIFE

ANN M. MARTIN

USBORNE

Night

The fire is crackling and my paws are warm. My tail, too, and my nose, my ears. I'm lying near the hearth on a plaid bed, which Susan bought for me. Lying in the warmth remembering other nights – nights in the woods under a blanket of stars, nights spent with Moon, nights in the shed when I was a puppy. And the many, many nights spent searching for Bone. The fire pops and I rise slowly, turn around twice, then a third time, and settle onto the bed again, Susan smiling fondly at me from her armchair.

Warmth is important to an old dog. At least it is to me. I can't speak for all dogs, of course, since not all dogs are alike. And most certainly, not all dogs have the same experiences. I've known of dogs who dined on fine foods and led pampered lives, sleeping on soft beds and being served hamburger and chicken and even steak. I've known of dogs who looked longingly at warm homes, who were not invited inside, who stayed in a garage or a shed or under a wheelbarrow for a few days, then moved on. I've known of dogs who were treated cruelly by human hands and dogs who were treated with the gentlest touch, dogs who starved and dogs who grew fat from too many treats.

I've known all these dogs, and I've been all these dogs.

Part One

The House in the Country

Lindenfield in the wintertime was a bleak place. The air was chill. For weeks on end a dog could see her breath all night long, and all day long as well. Even in early spring, as winter faded, the gardens, tended by humans in warm weather, were barren and silent. And the lakes and ponds were grey, and very still. No frogs croaked, no turtles sunned, no shiny fish twined through the underwater grasses. In warm weather, things would be different. The air would hum with insect noises, and the ponds might be quiet, but they were rarely silent. Along their muddy bottoms and on their banks and in the moss and grasses and fallen logs was a secret animal neighbourhood.

On the piece of land where the Merrions' big house rose from among gardens and walkways were all sorts of animal neighbourhoods. At the time I lived there, as a pup, there were the stone-wall neighbourhoods and the shed neighbourhoods and the garden neighbourhoods and the forest neighbourhoods and the pond neighbourhoods and the above-the-ground neighbourhoods. There was even a secret in-the-Merrions'-house neighbourhood. All were linked to form an animal world with the Merrions' house at the centre, like a stone that had been tossed in a pond. The further the ripples spread from the splash, the more animals were to be found, and the noisier and less secretive their lives were.

The time that I am talking about was not so very long ago, and yet it's my whole life ago. I haven't been back to the Merrions' house since the day I followed my brother off their property. In all my wandering I never found my way back there, but then of course, I was looking for Bone, not for the Merrions.

I really don't know much about the Merrions. I was very young when I lived on their land, and I was concentrating on what I needed to learn from Mother. But the Merrions couldn't be ignored. This is what I do know about them:

Their grand house, the house that was the centre of our world, was not the centre of the Merrions' world. In the spring, when Bone and I were born – in an old garden shed, the one with the unused chicken coop at the back – the Merrions lived in their house sporadically. They were not like most animals I knew, returning to their nests or burrows or holes night after night or, like the owls, day after day. Instead, they would arrive at the house, always in the evening, stay for a couple of days, then pile back into their car, drive down their lane, and turn onto the big road. Mother would watch as the car became smaller and smaller and finally disappeared. Then several entire nights and days would pass before the Merrions' car would pull into their lane again.

There were five Merrions in all. I understand that human children generally are not born in litters like puppies, but one or two at a time like deer. The two Merrion parents had given birth to three young. The oldest was a boy, then there was another boy, and finally a small girl, who was the loudest of the children. Over time I learned the names of the children, but only one mattered to me, and that was Matthias, the younger boy, the gentle one. But I did not know him until I was several months old.

The Merrions were tidy people. That was clear. Everything about their house and their property was tidy. The shutters hung straight and were repainted often. No toys littered the yard. The walks and the porches were swept clean, and the gardeners showed up regularly to edge the flower beds, mow the lawns, trim the hedges, and hang potted plants on the porches.

The Merrions did not own any pets. "Because of germs," Mother once told Bone and me. She had overheard Mrs Merrion talking to a gardener. "And hair," Mrs Merrion had added. "Germs and hair."

When Mother said this I thought of the in-the-Merrions'-house neighbourhood of animals. This consisted not only of many insects, but also of a large family of mice, two squirrels (in the attic walls), a possum who went in and out of the utility room through a hidden hole in the wall, and – in the basement – several snakes, two toads, and some lizards. There were plenty of germs and lots of hair in the Merrions' house, and this amused me. But I remembered the time I heard screaming and banging and crashing in the house and then Mr Merrion ran outside with a bag containing a dead, bleeding bat, which he shoved into a garbage can, and I did not feel so amused.

All the creatures on the property knew how the Merrions felt about animals, and they made their own decisions about where to live. Mother had her reasons for choosing the garden shed. There were other sheds and other small buildings on the property, each with its own population, each different from the others, each connected to, but separate from the Merrions.

And that is what I know about the Merrions at the time Bone and I were born. The days were mild – spring arrived early that year – and still the humans came to their home only for brief periods of time. An animal could live quite comfortably on the Merrion property. Around the house were nothing but woods and fields and rolling hills. The nearest neighbouring house was a good hour's trot away, for a grown dog. So the animal communities thrived. There were hawks and moths and foxes and fish and deer and owls and stray cats and frogs and spiders and possums and skunks and snakes and groundhogs and squirrels and chipmunks; birds and insects and non-human animals of all kinds.

Apart from Mother and Bone and me, the main residents in our garden shed were cats and mice. There were insects, too, but they were harder to get to know. They came and went and were very small.

The shed was a good place for cats and dogs. Mother chose well when she selected it as the spot in which to raise her puppies. It was a small wooden structure that had originally been built as a chicken coop, the nesting boxes still lining one end. The door was permanently ajar, and one window had been removed, which might have made the shed too cold for puppies and kittens. However, when the Merrions bought the big house, they planned to turn the shed into a playhouse for their children, and got as far as insulating two of the walls before Mrs Merrion decided that a chicken coop was unsanitary and better suited as a garden shed. So the Merrions built a brand-new playhouse and then a bigger garden shed, both sturdier than the chicken coop, and before long, they stopped using the old shed, except as a place in which to store things the gardeners rarely used.

Mother found the shed shortly before she gave birth to Bone and me. She was a stray dog – had never lived with humans, although she had lived around them – and had been roaming the hills and woods bordering the Merrions' property, looking for the right spot in which to give birth to her puppies. For several days she watched the Merrions' house from the edge of the woods. She watched the animals on the property, too. There were no other dogs that she could see, but there was a mother fox with four newly born kits, and sometimes, in the small hours of the morning, she heard coyotes yipping in the hills. Mother needed a place that was safe from predators, out of sight of the Merrions, and warm and dry for her puppies.

The shed seemed perfect. The first time she poked her nose through the partially open door she noticed how much warmer the inside air was than the spring air outside. She stood very still, listening and allowing her eyes to adjust to the darkness. She heard the scurrying of mice in straw, but nothing else.

The old nesting boxes for the chickens were along the wall across from the door. Mother had never seen anything like them. She crept forwards to investigate. First she surveyed them from several feet away. Then she crept closer, and finally she stuck her nose into one of the holes.

Hssss! Pttt! Something sprang out of the box, hissed and spat at Mother, then ducked inside again. It was a yellow cat, protecting a litter of newborn kittens. Mother backed up and surveyed the boxes from a little distance. Now she could see eyes in several of the holes. More cats. Mother left them alone. She was too big to fit in the boxes anyway. Behind her, along the sides of the shed and next to the door, were a few old gardening tools, some clay pots, a few piles of straw, and a wheelbarrow filled with burlap bags and more straw. The mice had chewed holes in the bags, but the burlap still looked cosy and warm. Mother glanced up. In the rafters above she could see several abandoned nests that had belonged to barn swallows and hornets.

Mother considered the cats again, the pairs of eyes glaring at her from the nesting boxes. And then she heard a tiny rustle behind her. She swept her head towards the door in time to see a large grey cat squeeze through it. The cat stared at Mother, then hurried by her and disappeared into a hole. Mother let out a quiet woof. In response, she heard a soft growl from the cat, but nothing more.

That afternoon Mother sat patiently near the door, watching the comings and goings of the cats. As long as she didn't move about too much, the cats kept their distance. Mother watched the mice, too. They kept their distance from the cats. When night fell, Mother crept to a pile of straw that was as far away from the cats as she could get. She curled up on it, her back to the nesting boxes, and fell asleep. She was safe, she was very warm, and the night passed peacefully.

In the morning, Mother felt she was ready to give birth to her puppies.

The Wheelbarrow

We were born in the wheelbarrow, Bone and I. Mother (her dog name was Stream, but to Bone and me she was simply Mother) managed to climb into it early that first morning, having decided that it was an ideal nest for her puppies.

Mother gave birth to five puppies, but only Bone and I survived. Two of the puppies were born dead, and a third lived for less than an hour. He was tiny, too tiny, and his legs were misshapen. Mother tossed him out of the wheelbarrow and ignored him. He whimpered several times, then was silent.

Bone and I were strong, though. We nuzzled into Mother and nursed from her. We squirmed and wiggled. We slept, our heads curled under our chests, we burrowed, we nursed some more. And when, after our first night, Mother saw that Bone and I were still strong and active and eating well, she gave us our names. She chose, as mother dogs do, names of things that are important to her. So I was known as Squirrel, and my brother was known as Bone.

My earliest memories are of warmth, comfort and food. For the first days of my life, my eyes and ears were not open. Bone and I slept most of that time, rousing ourselves only to eat. Awake or asleep we curled into our nest, into each other, and into Mother. I could feel the heartbeats of my brother and mother.

During this time, Mother left the wheelbarrow as little as possible, but she did have to leave it. She would rise unsteadily, cover Bone and me in the straw and burlap, climb over the edge of the wheelbarrow, and leave the shed to relieve herself and to find food. She would come back as soon as she could, and then Bone and I would squirm into her.

When Bone and I had been alive long enough for the moon to change from a disc to half a disc, our eyes and ears opened, and my world slowly became clear to me. Head and legs wobbling, I stood in the wheelbarrow and gazed around the shed. The light was dim but I could make out the nesting boxes and later the eyes that peered from within them.

All day long the adult cats came and went. When I wasn't sleeping, I followed their movements in the shed. The cats trotted back and forth, slinking through the open door. Sometimes they returned carrying small rodents in their mouths, sometimes birds. I watched them take their food back to the nesting boxes. The cats, sleek and lean and almost always hungry, would pause at the boxes and glance around the shed before leaping through a hole. They glanced around the shed before leaving the holes, too. Their glances always took in Mother. The shed cats were not our friends, but I think we trusted one another, even as wary as we all were.

One day, one of the shed cats, the hissing yellow one Mother had met when she first discovered the shed, left her kittens and did not return for a long, long time. By afternoon, her kittens were mewing loudly, so loudly that Mother jumped out of the wheelbarrow and poked her nose in their nesting box. I heard all sorts of spitting and growly noises from the adult cats in the shed, but Mother ignored them. She backed out of the box with a kitten in her mouth and dropped it to the floor. Then she pulled out two more kittens, lay on the floor beside them, and lifted her hind leg in the air. The kittens burrowed into Mother the way Bone and I did, searching for milk.

Creak. Behind us the shed door eased open. Standing in it was the yellow cat. She stared at Mother for a moment, then bolted through the shed. Mother leaped to her feet, the kittens tumbling away, and she scrambled back into our wheelbarrow while the cat collected her babies.

Our shed was busy all day long and all night long, too. Mother and Bone and I tended to sleep at night, but not the cats. And definitely not the mice. The mice were busy and noisy. We could hear them chewing. And climbing. There was no place in the shed the mice couldn't get to. They scurried up walls and posts and along rafters. They ran in and out of holes too tiny to notice. They emerged from unlikely places – under flowerpots and inside beams. Usually they could outrun the cats or escape from them, but sometimes a cat was smarter or more patient than a mouse, and then with a squeak, and a flash of teeth and claws, the mouse became a meal.

For a long time I felt secure as a dog, even a small one, in our shed. Mother was the biggest creature there, and she didn't fear the cats or the mice. But my eyes and ears had been open for just a few days when I realized what nearby threat Mother did fear, and that was the fox.

The fox, the one with the four kits, lived underneath the Merrions' new garden shed. I don't know where her mate was. I never saw him. And I wouldn't see the mother or her kits with my own eyes until the time that I was big enough and strong enough to leave the wheelbarrow and go outside. Mother saw the fox often, though. She paid attention to her and she even learned her name. Mother didn't learn the names of the other creatures on the Merrions' property, but the fox was a different story, and that was because Mother had recognized how dangerous she could be.

The fox's name was Mine, and I believe she had named herself. Mine wasn't interested in Mother. And she didn't know Mother had puppies, so Bone and I were not in danger from Mine. Still, Mother was afraid of her. Bone and I would peer over the edge of the wheelbarrow and see Mother at the door to the shed. She sat planted on her haunches, her brow creased, gazing out at the field beyond the Merrions' backyard. I could tell when Mine was in the field, because Mother sat at strict, grim attention. If a squirrel was out there, Mother would sit quivering, her tail twitching. She might even jump to her feet and give chase. But when Mine was outside, Mother watched motionless, except for the slow turn of her head as she tracked Mine from a garden to the woods, or from the playhouse to the Merrions' porch.

This was why Mother feared Mine: Mine had no sense. She didn't even have the sense to steer clear of the Merrions. She wandered through their yard at all hours, not caring who might see her. She didn't teach her kits to fear the Merrions, she didn't try to hide her kills, she was reckless, she was bold, she was cheeky. Mother thought Mine put us all in danger.

I didn't quite understand this, though, not when I was still such a young puppy that I couldn't leave our nest. All I knew then was life in our warm wheelbarrow, where each day was much the same as the next. Bone and Mother and I would lie in a pile of fur and feet and tails and snouts. Bone and I would nurse. When Mother left the shed, which she did more often as Bone and I grew older, I would peer over the edge of the wheelbarrow at the cats and mice. I watched the mice dart and hide, listened to them chew and squeak. I watched the cats come and go, listened to them mew and purr. Every now and then a cat or an older kitten would venture out of the shed and not return. I realize now what was happening: the mice were eating corn and seeds, the cats were eating the mice, and owls and hawks were eating the cats.

For the time being, I didn't have to worry about this, though, or about Mine. Mother fed me, Mother protected me, and I watched the world of the shed from our wheelbarrow island.

Mother

One day, when the shape of the moon had changed several times, and Bone and I were even bigger and stronger and steadier on our feet – a day when the air blew warm through the window of the shed and brought sweet fragrances to my nose, making it twitch – Mother nudged Bone and me over the edge of the wheelbarrow. She nudged Bone first because he was a boy, and then she nudged me. Bone landed on a stack of burlap sacks, and I landed on top of him. I looked up at Mother, at our little island, and I let out a whimper. But not Bone. Bone scampered to the floor. He spotted one of the cats and tried to pounce on her. The cat hissed, arched her back, and ran behind a stiff coil of hose. Bone wobbled after her, but stopped to sniff at a mousy-smelling flowerpot and forgot about the cat. Then, tail held high, he began to investigate the shed. I followed him. Mother followed us.

Soon Mother allowed Bone and me to investigate outside the shed, too, as long as we stayed out of view of the Merrions' house. The door to the shed faced across their yard. To one side was the back of their house; to the other were fields and woods. Bone and I were taught always to turn away from the house and hurry around the corner of the shed.

Behind the shed was much more interesting than in the shed. Behind the shed was Outdoors. Outdoors with birds and bugs and mice and moles. Outdoors with flowers and shrubs and bushes and trees. The more we investigated, the braver I felt, but only when Bone was in front of me. With Bone in front, his tail high, my own tail was held high. With Bone out of sight, I was lost.

Once Mother had tossed Bone and me off our island, our nest became the burlap bags on the floor below. Bone and I weren't big enough to scramble back up into the wheelbarrow. I think this worried Mother; she felt that the bed on the floor wasn't protected enough. Bone and I didn't care, though. We liked our freedom.

One morning, the air heavy and smelling of rain, Bone and I tumbled through the doorway, turned the corner, and began a game of chase behind the shed. We jumped, we yipped, we startled each other. We pounced, we ran, we practised growling. Bone had wrestled me to the ground when Mother appeared. She came towards us at a trot and lifted Bone off me by the scruff of his neck, then dragged him back to the shed. I followed.

Something was wrong.

Inside, Mother settled herself on our bed, but Bone and I were curious and peeped through the crack in the shed door. I could hear the voices of humans. Bone poked his nose all the way out the door then, and I ducked under him so I could see, too.

The Merrions' car was parked at the end of their lane. All the doors were open, and the Merrions were pulling out boxes and cases and carrying them into the house.

"We're here! We're here!" cried the girl in her very loud voice.

"For the whole summer," said one of the boys.

This was the first time that I could remember the Merrions coming back to their home when it wasn't night-time. In fact, the morning was barely over.

For a while, Bone and I watched the Merrions as they marched in and out of the house with their boxes and cases, but eventually we grew bored. We were stuck in the shed, though. Mother wouldn't let us leave it, not until all the Merrions were out of sight. Then she nosed us around the corner as fast as she could.

When I awoke the next morning, I found that the Merrions were still at their house. They were there the next day and the day after that and the day after that and for all the rest of the days I lived on their property. The games Bone and I played became quieter, no more yipping and woofing. But we weren't bored. Mother was busy teaching us things in the woods. She showed us how to hunt for small animals. She showed us how to mark our territory. She showed us how to fight and how to defend ourselves. And then one morning Mother left Bone and me playing beside a stone wall near our shed. She trotted off, looking as if she had a specific destination in mind. When she returned, she was carrying something wonderful smelling, but she wouldn't share it with us. With the

28

something still in her mouth, she turned and walked away, peering at us over her shoulder from time to time, keeping close to a row of bushes.

Bone knew what Mother wanted, and he followed her. So I followed Bone, as usual. The further I walked, the more my nose twitched. I could smell whatever Mother was carrying, and lots more.

Mother led us to garbage, to a lovely pile of things I had no names for at the time, but that I now know were old chicken and stale bread and bits of scrambled egg and several olives and some congealed spaghetti and a puddle of sour milk.

Bone and I pounced. This was how a dog could hunt even when there were no animals to hunt for. This was heaven.

That night, our stomachs full of scraps, Bone and I lay curled up in the shed with Mother. It was a rainy night and the wind blew and thunder growled and every now and again bright light would flash through cracks in the ceiling. I nuzzled against Mother and was beginning to doze when I heard a noise outside, a noise that wasn't part of the storm.

Yip, yip, yip!

It sounded faint and far away.

Mother and Bone were fast asleep, but I wanted to know what was outside. I crept off the burlap sacks and across the shed to the open door. I peered into darkness. I can see well in the dark, but with the storm I could make out little until the next flash of lightning turned the yard to noontime, and there was Mine. I glimpsed her only for a second. She was standing, dripping, at the Merrions' back door. What was she doing? Hoping to find food? Surely she knew where the garbage heap was.

I waited for the next flash of lightning, and when it came Mine had vanished. I watched our yard until the storm moved away and there was only the dark and the rain. Then I returned to our bed and the heartbeats of Mother and Bone.

Mother had known Mine meant trouble, and now I knew it, too. It was as if Mine were an alien creature in our world, and didn't know our ways. But over the next few days, I almost forgot about her. I didn't see her or her kits. The rain had ended and the Merrion children spent a lot of time playing in their yard. Because the children were outside, Bone and I needed to be more cautious than ever.

We were also entertained. If we couldn't play, at least we could watch the Merrion children play.

And we did. The older boy and the little girl shrieked. They ran. They climbed onto large wheeled toys, which I later learned were called bicycles, and rode them up and down their lane. The younger boy was quieter. He didn't come outside as often as his brother and sister, and when he did, he mostly sat under a tree.

Sometimes Mrs Merrion stood on one of the porches and called to her children: "Put your shoes back on! I don't want you outside barefoot!" "Don't go in the flower beds. The gardeners were just here!" "Matthias, please, take your nose out of that book and get some exercise. It's too nice to sit around and read all day!"

Bone and I were fascinated, even if we missed playing our own games.

And then one evening I saw Mine again. She trotted through the Merrions' yard at sunset, just as the girl ran outside calling, "I want to catch fireflies before I go to bed, okay?" She held a glass jar in her hand.

I'm not sure whom she was talking to. Mother and Bone and I were in the shed, and I was peeking out the door, but I didn't have a view of the entire yard. I heard the scream, though. All the animals on the property heard it. The girl had said she wanted to catch fireflies, and then someone let out a scream as loud as a screech owl or a raccoon, and then Mrs Merrion shouted, "It's a fox! A fox is in our yard! Come inside!"

Mine bolted. I saw her tear across the yard and disappear into the woods.

It was the next night, at about the same time, when Mother and Bone and I heard human voices outside the door to our shed. I hadn't been around the humans often enough then to be able to recognize who was speaking, but I thought I heard Mrs Merrion. And I heard the voice of another grown male who might have been one of the gardeners. I didn't have time to puzzle over this, though. Mother grabbed me and dragged me through the shed towards the nesting boxes, Bone at our heels. From inside the boxes came low growls of warning, but Mother ignored them. She nosed Bone and me into the darkest corner of the shed and stood in front of us facing the door.

My heart thumped so hard I could feel it beating in my throat. I sat trembling behind Mother, waiting for the shed door to bang open, but I heard only the sound of voices.

"That fox is a menace. My wife thinks it's rabid."

"Well, I—"

"Are you sure you know how to handle that thing?"

"I never miss my mark."

"I know where the fox's den is."

"There's not going to be enough light to take care of this tonight."

The voices faded away. My heart stopped pounding.

The next afternoon I was following Bone to the garbage heap when I heard an explosion. It was so loud that it echoed through the hills and startled the birds, who fell silent.

Bone and I looked at each other in all that quiet, then turned to run back to the shed, but we skidded to a halt when we saw one of the gardeners. He was trotting across the yard towards the furthest flower bed, and he was carrying a rifle. I let my eyes travel ahead of him to the garden.

There was Mine. She lay in a heap under a peony plant. She was very still.

Mother found Bone and me then and herded us towards the shed, staying well away from the men. As soon as the gardener bent over to look at Mine, Mother ran us around the corner and pushed us through the door, and we retreated to the dark corner again.

The rest of the day was quiet. We didn't leave the shed. And we didn't see or hear the Merrion children. But all afternoon Mine's kits yipped softly in their den.

Early the next morning Mother left the shed and trotted off in the direction of the garbage heap.

She never came back.

Secret Dogs

Bone and I waited a very long time for Mother. That first morning, when we didn't know that she wasn't coming back, we entertained ourselves as we usually did. We hunted in the woods. We played by the stone wall. We visited the garbage heap and found bits of smoked turkey, a melon rind, coffee grounds (which we tasted but didn't like) and half a piece of cake with white frosting. We ate until our stomachs were quite fat.

The day was very hot. It was so hot that the Merrion children, who had been spraying one another with the garden hose in the morning, went indoors for their lunch and didn't come back outside. By the time the sun had reached its highest point and had started to pass over the Merrions' backyard, the shed, even with its open window and door, had grown too stuffy for any creatures except the mice. Bone and I lay in the shade of the woods and waited for Mother.

At the end of the day, when the shadows were long and the heat had faded a bit, Bone and I returned to the shed. I expected to find Mother in our nest. Sometimes now Mother left us for long periods of time, but she always came back by evening. Our nest was empty, though. And the shed was still stuffy. One of the cats poked his head through the door, sniffed at the dusty, dense air, turned and left. Bone and I remained. I was hungry and I suspect Bone was, too, but we wanted Mother.

The air cooled, darkness fell, the stars came out and so did the bats, and still Mother did not appear. Bone and I curled into each other in our nest, our stomachs rumbling. I thought of the garbage heap, of the turkey and melon rind and cake, but Bone and I hadn't been outside in the night-time by ourselves yet. Besides, surely Mother was on her way back to us.

All that night Bone and I slept on the burlap sack,

slept with our legs and tails entwined. I could feel Bone's breath on my neck. It was our first night without Mother, and it seemed very long. In the morning when I awoke I saw Bone, three of the shed cats, and a mouse poking its head out of a flowerpot, but no Mother, I knew that she was not going to come back at all.

Bone and I were on our own. We were responsible for finding all of our food and water, and for remembering the many, many things Mother had taught us – how to stay out of trouble, when to snap and bite at an animal, to steer clear of humans and other dogs, to clean our wounds, to groom ourselves. We tried hard and we managed fairly well. The garbage heap became our best friend.

I do not understand emotions very well. I know what fear feels like, and I have been afraid many times. But I am less clear about words such as joy, happiness, sadness and anger. Over the years I have heard humans, especially Susan, talk about these things, though, and I see how Susan appears when she says she is happy. Looking back, I think I was happy during the rest of that summer when Bone and I lived in the shed; that I was happy even though Mother was gone.

The truth was that with Mine gone as well, the Merrions' property was a much more peaceful place and our world seemed less threatening. Mine's kits had left, too – the morning after their mother was killed they tumbled out of their den, trotted into the woods, and just kept going. So the Merrions' yard was free of foxes, and I was not to see the man with the gun for quite a while. Bone and I began to feel safe.

The air cooled down after that one blistering day, and sometimes I saw the Merrion children wearing the kind of clothes they had worn in the spring. Cooler air meant that the shed was more comfortable. And just enough rain fell – enough to fill the buckets and watering cans that Bone and I drank from, but not so much that we couldn't go hunting. We were not very experienced hunters yet, my brother and I, but we caught enough small animals here and there so that our stomachs were usually full. If we had a bad day, we could always raid the garbage heap.

Our lives were quiet. Bone and I played and hunted. We chased squirrels and chipmunks and each other. I finally made friends with some of the shed cats. One of them, Yellow Man, would wait for me in front of the nesting boxes each morning and rub his head under my chin before he left to spend the day in the woods. I even came to recognize the shed mice, every single one of them. I never thought of them as meals.

They were my neighbours.

It was a warm afternoon with the smell of cut grass in the air and bees humming in the bushes when Matthias discovered Bone and me. He took us by surprise. We had eaten breakfast at the garbage heap and were napping in the woods, our bellies full, when I heard the sound of crunching leaves and a hushed human voice. Bone and I jerked to attention. Here came Matthias, the boy who liked to sit under trees, the boy Mrs Merrion would tell to take his nose out of that book. He was carrying a book now, and talking to himself, and his face looked like Susan's does after Mrs Oliver has told her she's too old to be living on her own.

Bone and I drew back and held very still, afraid to run and draw attention to ourselves.

Matthias almost stepped on us.

"Hey!" he cried. "What – hey, I found puppies!"

Bone and I did scramble away then. We ran straight for the shed and zipped through the door.

Matthias ran after us and followed us to our nest.

"Hey, puppies. Hey, puppies," he said. "I won't hurt you." He held his hand towards us.

Bone growled at it.

"I know. You don't trust me," said Matthias. "I don't blame you. You don't know me." He paused. "Not yet anyway."

Bone and I left our nest then and backed into a corner.

Matthias stood up but he didn't approach us. "I'll be right back," he said.

As soon as Matthias left the shed, Bone and I scooted out the door and ran for the woods.

We hid in the woods, afraid to move about, but by the end of the day we felt brave enough to make our way to the garbage heap. When we did, I saw Matthias walking around the Merrions' yard. He was holding something in his hand, and he was peering under bushes and around trees and in the sheds and playhouse. He didn't call out, though, as Mr and Mrs Merrion had done one day when they couldn't find the noisy little girl. I realize now that Matthias didn't want his mother to know he had found puppies on the property. She wouldn't stand for that. We were Matthias's secret.

We didn't want to be Matthias's secret, though. Mother had taught Bone and me to fear humans, so we tried to stay alert and keep out of Matthias's way. But one morning the rains came again, and after Bone and I had found breakfast and relieved ourselves, we returned to the shed. We were settling in for a cosy day with Yellow Man, the rain drumming on the roof, when the door was flung open and in walked Matthias.

"There you are," he said softly when he saw Bone and me.

Matthias always spoke softly, not like his sister. He crouched down and held out his hand.

I glanced over my shoulder. Yellow Man and the other cats had retreated to the furthest recesses of the nesting boxes. I was about to run for the corner when a scent, a wonderful, beautiful scent, reached my nose.

Chicken.

Matthias was offering us pieces of chicken.

Bone and I couldn't bring ourselves to approach Matthias, but we didn't turn and run, either.

Matthias stretched his hand out as far as it would reach.

Bone and I darted forwards to snatch the chicken, and then we did retreat to the corner.

Matthias grinned. "That's all for today," he said. And he left.

But he returned with more chicken the next morning and the next morning and many mornings after that. By the third morning, Bone and I didn't feel that we needed to hide in the corner in order to eat our prizes. Matthias did nothing while we ate but sit and wait and watch. If Susan had been there then, she would have said that Matthias was patient.

One morning Bone and I were eating our fabulous chicken breakfasts when I realized that Matthias's hand was resting on my back. His other hand was resting on Bone's back. I was startled, but not so startled that I couldn't finish the chicken.

The following morning, Matthias stroked our heads while we ate.

And then one morning he pulled me into his lap. I struggled at first, but Matthias kept patting me and murmuring, "You're such a good puppy. The best puppy ever. Good puppy, good puppy." He pulled Bone into his lap next, and Bone growled, but he didn't struggle too much.

After that, I waited every morning for Matthias to

come to the shed. Sometimes Bone waited, too, sometimes he didn't. Matthias always brought chicken, and sometimes he brought a ball or a toy. I would eat the chicken and then I would sit in Matthias's lap. Or we would play in the grass behind the shed. I noticed that Matthias was as careful to stay out of sight of his house as Bone and I were.

At the height of summer, something of autumn was already in the air – although I didn't realize it then, didn't know that the days would turn short and cold and that food would become hard to find. It was during this time that Bone and I saw the man with the gun again. And one evening we heard a blast from the rifle.

Bone stayed awake all the rest of that night. I had seen him do this on other nights, had watched as he woke from a deep sleep, sat up, and listened to the coyotes in the hills or to voices from the Merrions' porch. My brother was becoming restless. I loved our summer days – being greeted by Yellow Man in the morning, hunting or going to the garbage heap with Bone, waiting for Matthias, romping in the woods. But Bone was tiring of our days. And he was becoming suspicious. He eyed the Merrions, even Matthias, more warily than ever. He growled when he saw the man with the gun. And on the morning after the rifle blast, he decided to leave our home in the country.

The Highway

Very early on the morning after the shotgun blast, when the night-time creatures were going to sleep and the humans hadn't awakened yet, Bone rolled off our burlap bed, touched my nose with his, then slipped through the open door of the shed and out into the quiet. I stood in the doorway watching him and saw that he looked at me over his shoulder from time to time. He trotted along the row of bushes and paused at the garbage pile, but when he kept going, I knew he was leaving for good.

I turned and looked behind me at the shed. I looked at the nesting boxes sheltering Yellow Man and the other sleeping cats and kittens, at the wheelbarrow that had been my first nest, at the mice and their hiding places. I looked around at it all, glowing a bit in the rising sun. The shed was my home. It was everything I knew.

But Bone was leaving.

So I ran after him.

I was too young then to wonder what would happen at the shed that day without us. But now I think I know. Yellow Man would rise and stretch, creep out of his box, and sniff the air. He would wait for me, wait to rub his head under my chin, but our nest would be empty and I wouldn't come tumbling back from the woods or the garbage heap, so finally he would prowl around outside alone. He would look for me off and on for many days and then he would forget about me.

The shed mice would forget about us almost immediately. They would register that Bone and I were gone, and then they would continue with their foraging and eating and running about as if we had never lived in the shed in the first place.

Matthias would never forget. I am fairly certain of that. I imagine that Matthias searched his yard for us for more days than Yellow Man did. He must have searched quietly, holding out his chicken and toys; searched the entire property, and then maybe even ventured off the property. And knowing what I have learned about emotions, I think he was probably sad for a very long time.

If I had imagined these things when I was a puppy, though – if I had imagined Yellow Man waiting and Matthias searching – I would still have run after Bone. The shed might have been my home, and Yellow Man and Matthias might have been my companions, but without Mother, Bone was my world. I could not be separated from him.

So I ran after my brother. I ran hard, yipping to let him know I was coming. Bone heard me, and waited for me to catch up. Then we trotted along shoulder to shoulder until I realized I was as far from the shed as I had ever been. Behind me I could see the Merrions' house, its chimneys and roofs among the tallest tree branches, swallows swooping by the attic windows. We hurried on. The next time I looked behind me, I could see only the chimney tops. The third time I looked, the house was gone.

Bone and I made our way down a steep hill, stumbling through dense, dark woods. Then we walked along flatter terrain; walked and walked until I began to feel hungry, and I thought of the garbage pile, and of fat rodents. I was thirsty, too, and presently Bone and I came to a stream and stood at the edge and took long drinks. Then we waded in. We were hot and the water was cold, and we could see small dark shapes darting back and forth just below the surface. Bone stared at the fish for a moment, then pounced on one with a large splash. I pounced, too. We didn't catch anything, but pouncing was fun. And it made Bone frisky. He turned and ran at me, chasing me up the stream as far as a small waterfall. At the waterfall we waded to the bank and continued through the woods.

We kept the sun first at our fronts, then at our backs, as it moved through the sky. By the time the day's heat was fading and the shadows felt cooler, our stomachs were rumbling, so we hunted. Then we rested. And then abruptly Bone stood up and trotted off.

I followed him.

This time Bone and I walked and walked until the trees became fewer and we could see their separate shadows, and the shadows were long. Finally there were no more trees, and we were walking through a field, and then I heard a swishing noise that reminded me of the sound of cars on the road to the Merrions' house.

Bone heard the noise, too, and he stopped. He froze in place and his ears stood up stiffly as he listened.

The noise meant cars, I was sure of it, even though the whooshes weren't exactly the same as the ones at the Merrions'. They were louder and quicker. *WHOOSH-WHOOSH-WHOOSH-WHOOSH.*

I watched Bone. He began to walk again, more slowly. We saw an abandoned tractor in the field and made a wide circle around it. We saw a rabbit and Bone ran at it, but the rabbit disappeared.

WHOOSH-WHOOSH-WHOOSH. Where were all those cars I could hear?

Bone, panting from his chase, stopped to catch his breath, and it was then that we saw the house. It was smaller than the Merrions', and sat at the edge of the field, tidy and somehow friendly looking, but Bone and I turned away from it and walked in the other direction. We walked until the field came to an end and in front of us was a road, a highway. And there were the whooshes. One car after another zipped along the road. The cars went by so fast they looked blurry, and even when Bone and I retreated to the edge of the field, each car blew our ears back with a rush of hot wind as it sped by.

I squinted my eyes against the dust and the wind and turned around. We could creep through the field again, avoid the house, and return to the woods where we could hunt. I was partway along a row of tall, scratchy plants when I realized that Bone wasn't with me. He was still standing at the side of the road. And he was sniffing the air. An odour came to my nose. I sniffed, too.

Chicken – just like Matthias would bring us. The odour was coming from across the road. I ran back to Bone, strained to see past the rushing cars, and when there was a little break in the traffic, I saw a paper bag lying on its side.

There was chicken in that bag, and Bone and I knew it. My mouth started to water and I drooled as I stood at the edge of the field, separated from the chicken by two lanes of cars.

Bone took a step forwards, then another. I was right behind him, but when a truck whizzed by me, I jumped back, yelping. Bone glanced at me, then faced the traffic again. He looked as though he were getting ready to run – to bolt across the road and hope for the best – when suddenly one of the cars that had just sped by pulled to the side of the road and screeched to a stop. Other drivers honked their horns, but the people who had stopped, a woman and a man, ignored them. They jumped out of the car and ran to Bone and me. Bone still had his eyes on that bag of chicken, but I was watching the people, and I wanted to get away from them. I couldn't leave Bone, though.

I let out a warning bark.

Too late. The man scooped Bone into his arms, and the woman scooped me into her arms.

"Look, they're just puppies," the woman exclaimed. "What are they doing way out here?"

The man looked sternly at Bone. "You guys could have gotten yourselves killed," he said. "This is a dangerous highway."

"Well, honey, they don't know any better," said the woman. "They're little. They must have gotten lost."

"Do they have any collars or tags?" asked the man, feeling around Bone's neck.

Bone stiffened, jerked his head over his shoulder, and snapped at the man.

The man almost dropped him. "Hey!" he shouted. "You little brat! Don't do that again." He gave Bone a shake.

"George, I just told you, they don't know any better," said the woman. "Come on, let's get back in the car. It's not safe standing out here."

I squirmed. The woman's hands around my body were not gentle, as Matthias's had been. She held me too tightly, and it was hard to breathe. I looked desperately at Bone, who was struggling and twisting and growling as the man, George, held him at arm's length.

"They're scrappy," said the woman brightly.

"They're a pain in the neck," George replied. He tucked Bone under one arm while he opened the car door. "Stick them in the back, Marcy," he said. "That way they won't pee on us." He paused. "What are we going to do with them, anyway?"

"Keep them! They're cute. They'll settle down. They're probably just scared."

This was true. Bone and I were petrified. We huddled on the floor of the car behind George and Marcy. I whimpered and whined, and the movement of the car made my stomach roll.

"Here we are!" Marcy said presently.

The car turned a corner and I threw up.

"Blasted creatures," said George. "Now the car is going to stink to high heaven."

"I'll clean it up," said Marcy. She peered over the seat at Bone and me. "Welcome to your new home."

Bad Dogs

I didn't want a new home. I wanted the shed. I wanted Mother. I wanted the garbage heap. I wanted Yellow Man and the mice and Matthias. I wanted Bone and me curled up on our burlap nest. When Bone had walked away from our shed that morning, I hadn't thought about *why*. Was it to escape a place he felt was dangerous? Was it to search for a safe new home? I wouldn't have left, but Bone had chosen to. Maybe he had a reason, maybe not. It didn't matter, because here were George and Marcy carrying us to their house and they were making the choices now.

Marcy unlocked the door to our new home. The house

was smaller than the Merrions' and bigger than the little one at the edge of the field, but with hardly any space between it and the house on either side. And all along the road were houses, houses and more houses, each with a flat yard in front, planted with spindly trees.

Marcy opened the door, stepped into a cool dark room, and placed me on the floor. "There you go," she said to me. "Let's get you cleaned up."

I licked at the foam around my mouth as George carried Bone inside and set him on the floor next to me. I looked miserably at Bone. My stomach was sloshing around like the stream we had played in, and I needed to pee. In our shed home, we were careful not to pee in our nest (we rarely even peed in the shed), so I stepped delicately off the rug Bone and I were standing on, squatted, and peed on the floor by the door.

"Hey!" shouted George. "Bad dog! *Bad* dog! Stop that!" He grabbed me up, pee dribbling from between my legs, shoved the front door open, and tossed me onto the steps.

From inside I could hear Bone let out a high-pitched angry bark, and Marcy say, "George, calm *down*."

I wasn't sure what I was supposed to do out there on the steps. I had finished peeing, and I wanted to get away from George and Marcy, but Bone was still in the house. So I sat trembling before the door until Marcy opened it and brought me inside again.

"Now, look here," she said as she herded Bone and me into a large room with a table in the centre and no rug on the floor. "You can't pee indoors. Do you understand? *No peeing!*"

"Marcy, for heaven's sake, they don't know what you're saying," George called. He was in the other room, swishing a rag over the puddle I had made. "And they're not house-trained. I hope you realize that. They're not house-trained. Do you really want the job of house-training two puppies?"

"How difficult can it be?" Marcy called back to him. "They're young. This is when you're supposed to teach them."

She looked down and saw Bone lifting his leg against a wooden chair, saw me pooping in a corner of the room, and quietly swatted each of us on our bottoms.

Then she hissed, "*Bad* dogs!" in a voice not loud enough for George to hear, and cleaned up our messes quickly.

Bone and I retreated under the table and hid among a maze of chair legs. After Marcy had finished cleaning up, she said, "Okay! Suppertime!" and fished under the table for us. Bone let out a long low growl, while I backed away from her.

"Go ahead, growl if you want," said Marcy, wounded. She stood up. "You'll come out when I offer you food."

"What are you going to feed them?" asked George. He entered the room with a fistful of soggy paper towels.

Marcy was opening and closing cabinets. "Well, I'll get them some dog food tomorrow. For now they can eat —"

I didn't hear what Marcy was going to suggest, because at that moment George lifted the lid on a garbage can, and Bone shot out from under the table, knocked the can over, and pounced on the food scraps.

I forgot about my misery when I smelled all those familiar odours — eggs and sausage and cookie crumbs and apple peelings. I forgot about my stomach, too. I was hungry, I was starving, and here was another garbage heap. I snatched at a piece of turkey, and Bone whisked a stale piece of bread – a whole piece! – under the table and ate it in big gulps, growling all the while.

"No, *no*, NO!" George shouted. "Marcy, will you *look* at this mess."

Marcy yanked the can upright and tried to gather the

spilled garbage into a heap, while Bone and I kept darting out from under the table to grab at more bits of food.

"No!" Marcy yelled again and again. "Bad dogs!"

Bone and I didn't settle down until we were full of food scraps. Then we fell asleep under the table.

I knew that at some point Marcy slid my brother and me out from under the table. She did this gently, saying, "Oh, tired puppies, tired puppies. Look how sleepy you are."

I knew she and George sat on the kitchen floor for a long time, Bone in her lap, me in George's.

I knew these things, and Bone knew these things, but after our day of travelling we were suddenly so tired we couldn't even open our eyes.

"Tired puppies," Marcy murmured again, stroking Bone's back.

George stroked my back and now his hand – the one that had flung me out the door – felt more like Matthias's.

"How old do you think they are?" Marcy whispered to George.

George continued stroking my back. "I don't know. They must be several months old at least. I don't think they're *baby* babies. Maybe five months?"

"Still pretty young," said Marcy. "We'll have to get

them to the vet soon. We don't even know if they're boys or girls." She paused. "I wonder what they're doing on their own."

"They're probably feral, you know," George replied. "I don't think they've lived with people before."

I fell sound asleep then. I didn't waken until I felt myself being lifted up and carried somewhere. I opened my eyes and found that George and Marcy were settling Bone and me in a large box in that room with no rug. The box was lined with newspapers.

"This will be your bed tonight," said Marcy. She patted us on our heads. "Tomorrow we'll get you something better. Goodnight, puppies."

The room went dark and I could hear footsteps trail up and away from us. For a long time I tried to nestle into Bone, to curl into him and pretend we were safely tucked into our burlap bed. But I needed to pee and I missed the rustling of the mice and the soft sighs and mews of Yellow Man and the cats. I listened hard for anything familiar, for owls or even coyotes. I thought I heard some faint cricket songs, but that was all.

I edged away from Bone. I had to pee desperately now, but I didn't want to go in our bed. Bone was restless, too, and probably needed to pee just as desperately as I did.

I let out a whimper. Bone let out a louder whimper. I whined. And then Bone started to howl. I joined him, and we howled and cried until suddenly the room grew bright and there stood Marcy, her hands on her hips.

"What on earth is wrong?" she exclaimed. "For heaven's sake, be quiet, puppies."

Bone and I stood up, resting our front feet against the sides of the box. We jumped and yipped and whimpered.

Marcy glanced over her shoulder. "It is *two o'clock* in the *morning*," she said fiercely. "Please. You have to be quiet."

My bladder was about to burst. I barked sharply.

"Okay. That does it." Marcy dragged the box out of the room, down a short hallway, and into a small space. "If you can't be quiet, you'll have to spend the night here in the laundry room." I heard a click, the room became dark, and Marcy left, slamming the door behind her.

Bone and I cried some more, and then I finally peed in a corner of our box. Bone peed where I had peed. Now our box was wet and it was smelly, but we were exhausted again, so at last we fell asleep.

* * *

When Bone and I lived in the shed we woke slowly each morning as the rays of the sun crept through the windows and lightened our home. When I awoke in the laundry room I had no idea whether morning had come. The room was as black as midnight.

I sat up in our stinky box and poked my nose into Bone. He whimpered and turned over. I heard a noise then, a small thump, and Marcy opened the door.

"Morning, puppies," she whispered. "I see you finally settled down." Marcy reached into the box and was stroking me when Bone woke suddenly, saw the large hand on his sister's back, darted forwards, and bit the hand.

"Ow! Stop it!" cried Marcy. She slapped Bone across his nose and stood up fast. Bone yelped.

"Marcy? What is it?" called George.

"The brown puppy just bit me."

George appeared in the doorway. "Okay. That does it. Those puppies go today. We don't need this, Marcy."

"No, no, please. Just give them one more chance."

George scowled. "Forget it."

"No, really. One more chance."

George shook his head.

Bone and I didn't know what another chance was, but if we had, we wouldn't have wanted it. In any case, we lost the chance. The moment Marcy carried us, very gingerly, back to the room where we had eaten our dinner of stolen scraps, Bone squirmed out of her grasp, tore across the floor to another pail of garbage, wrestled it over, and began tossing bits of food to me.

Marcy looked helplessly at George and said, "I have to leave for work now."

"Great. So this is my mess to clean up?"

"I'm sorry. I can't help it. I—"

"Never mind. Just go."

Marcy looked at Bone and me, started to say something, then turned and left the room.

As soon as my brother and I had stopped growling and eating, George stuffed us into a carton, smaller than the one we had spent the night in, tossed the carton onto the front seat of his car, started the engine with a roar, and drove away very fast.

The Throwaways

George drove so fast that when he turned corners I could hear the car squeal, and Bone and I would tumble against the sides of the box. My heart began to pound. I panted and licked my lips and tried to ignore the rolling in my stomach.

Every now and then I could hear George mutter things like, "Blasted dogs" or "What was Marcy *think*ing?" or "…ought to have her head examined."

The car turned another corner and this time I could feel the box slide across the seat and into George's side. He whacked it with the flat of his hand, catching Bone's jaw from the other side and causing him to yelp.

"Shut up, you little pills," said George loudly, and he whacked the box again, this time knocking me in the head. I was too stunned to yelp. The whack sent me flying into a corner of the box, and I huddled there silently.

Presently the car slowed down. I could hear sounds from George's side of the seat, but I couldn't see what he was doing. After a moment our box was opened roughly, and then...and then I watched as George, sweating, yanked Bone up by the scruff of his neck and tossed him through the open window of the car. No sooner had Bone disappeared from sight, than George grabbed me up in the same manner, threw me out the window, gunned the engine of his car, and sped away.

Bone landed hard, his snout smashing against pavement, and he couldn't help letting out another cry of pain. I landed a little distance away from him, on my shoulder, and I heard a small crack, but again I was too stunned to yelp. After a moment, I tried to stand, though. I staggered up on my hind legs first, then onto my uninjured front leg. But when I put weight on the other leg, it gave way and I sank down again.

I looked at Bone. He was limping towards me, his nose bloody, and he had almost reached me when I heard someone cry, "Did you see that? Some guy threw those puppies out of a car!"

"Are they all right?" asked someone else.

I glanced around. Bone and I had landed on asphalt, like the Merrions' lane, only this piece of asphalt was much, much bigger. And cars were lined up on it as far as I could see. Ahead of me was a row of buildings, which people kept hurrying in and out of.

The people who had spotted Bone and me were two women, their arms loaded with heavy bags. They ran to us now, set the bags on the asphalt, and knelt down.

"I think they're going to be okay," said one.

"Look how cute this one is," said the other, motioning to Bone. "The brown one. I always wanted a puppy. I'm going to take it home."

"What about the spotted one?"

"Well, I don't think I can manage two dogs, and that one isn't as cute. I'll just take this one."

"And leave the other one here?"

"It'll be all right. Someone else will come along and find it. That's why they were dumped at the mall, you know."

The women gathered up their bags and walked off

with a struggling, squirming Bone, wiping his nose with a Kleenex as they went.

Bone was gone. I was separated from my brother. I tried to run after the women, but I couldn't keep up with them. The pain in my shoulder made me sit down. I tipped my head back and let out a long low howl.

For a while I rested on the asphalt, but it was sticky and hot and hard against my rump, and I didn't like sitting among so many cars. Tentatively I stood up, keeping my injured leg off the ground. I found that I could move around on three legs, and I made my way off the asphalt to the shade of a tree on a little spit of grass with a lamp post planted in it. I rested again for a while, dozed off, and when I awoke I tried standing on all fours. It hurt, but I could do it. I could walk on my injured leg, too.

I was thirsty, so I looked around for a brook or a stream. I didn't see either one, but I found a puddle at the edge of the asphalt and had a drink from that.

Mother had taught Bone and me to be wary of people. But I was also wary of cars now, and with so many of them around I was afraid to move. I returned to the tree and made myself very still and small under it.

All afternoon I watched people and cars come and go. No one noticed me. The light began to fade, and I felt chilly. I was used to cuddling up with Bone for warmth, and now he was gone. I sidled over to the tree and tried cuddling up among its roots, but they were cool and rough and unyielding.

I sat up and found that I was shivering. For a while, shaking, I watched the cars. I noticed that more were leaving than were arriving. The asphalt was becoming emptier and emptier. I noticed the quiet, too. At midday, with the sun high in the sky, the air had been filled with voices, the rustle of bags, the blare of car horns, and music floating through the open windows of some of those cars. Now I heard only occasional quiet voices as people left the row of buildings and drove away.

By the time darkness fell, just a few cars were left, the asphalt stretching away from me like a great black pond. And still I sat shivering under the tree. I was cold, I was tired, my shoulder ached, and I was hungry. I was very, very hungry.

With a sigh, wondering where Bone was, wondering where Mother was, I took another drink from the puddle. Mother was truly gone; I felt sure of that. Something had happened and she had died. That was the only reason she would have left Bone and me when we were so young. But Bone…Bone could be somewhere nearby. Maybe he had a home with the woman with all the bags; maybe he didn't. After all, our first home with people hadn't worked out. Maybe Bone had escaped from the woman and was looking for me right now. Maybe he was trying to make his way back to this place where we had been thrown away.

I should wait for Bone, I thought, but I couldn't stay here. The water in the puddle wouldn't last, and I needed food. I looked all around me, straining my eyes to notice any movement, and saw the last car drive away. I sniffed the air. I smelled exhaust, car tyres, the soles of people's shoes, squirrel, mouse, insect, something like mouse but not *exactly* mouse, dog pee (not mine), and something sweet. I sat up as tall as I could and stretched my nose as high as it would go.

Sniff, sniff, sniff.

Was that garbage I smelled? Cautiously, I stepped away from the tree, stepped off the spit of grass, and began to cross the asphalt. Garbage was my best chance for a meal.

I followed my nose in and out of pools of light from the lamp posts.

Sniff, sniff, sniff.

I came to a bit of hamburger bun and snapped it up. I came to a paper cup lying on its side and lapped up the white liquid that had run out of it. I came to some crunchy yellow bits and tasted them. Salty.

This was fine, but I knew I smelled more garbage. Garbage like the Merrions' garbage heap. Real garbage.

I found it behind the buildings the people had been going in and out of. A whole row of garbage cans. Most of the lids were fastened tightly, but one can had been tipped over and its lid had popped off.

Dinner!

I dived into the can and was rooting through it, had just caught the scent of turkey, when I heard a low growl behind me. I backed out of the can and without even turning to see what was growling, I ran.

I ran and ran, across the empty stretch of asphalt, in and out of the lamplight, past puddles, past tempting mouthfuls of food. I ran until the asphalt ended and I crossed a stretch of grass. Then I screeched to a stop. Before me was a line of whizzing, whooshing cars, all with two bright eyes shining on their fronts, and I remembered Bone and the busy road the day before.

Panting, I glanced over my shoulder. I saw no growling thing, but I wasn't eager to turn back. I looked at the cars again.

WHOOSH-WHOOSH-WHOOSH-WHOOSH-WHOOSH-WHOOSH. This road was different from the other one, though. It wasn't busy all the time. Cars would speed by, then the street would become dark and silent. No cars. Then WHOOSH-WHOOSH-WHOOSH again. I waited. The next time the whooshing stopped and I couldn't see any car eyes, I tore across the road. On the other side I found more grass. And then I found trees. Lots of trees. A little woods.

When I turned around and peered through the trees, I could just make out the eyes on the cars. When I looked in the other direction, I saw only woods. I could have been behind the Merrions' house. I made my way through the darkness, listening to familiar sounds – to crickets, to the small chirpings of birds, to a pair of owls calling to each other.

I fell asleep that night on a nest of dry leaves, my stomach mostly empty, my mouth dry, my shoulder throbbing. I wished for our old bed in the wheelbarrow, wished for Bone, wished to hear Mother's heartbeat.

Part Two

Squirrel Alone

The woods became my home. I stayed there for a long time – for as long as it takes the leaves on the trees to turn from green (a colour I can't see, but I have heard Susan and other people talk of green leaves and green grass and other things that are green) to yellow, then drop off; for the snows to fall, then melt; and for my legs to grow long. Since I was still a puppy, all those things were new to me. I didn't know that the leaves would fall off the trees as the air grew colder. I didn't know that in the coldest weather of all snow would fall instead of leaves, covering the ground and making food harder to find. I didn't know that as the air warmed again the leaves would return, green like caterpillars. And I hadn't realized I was growing. I knew only that everything was new to me, and that being an independent puppy was difficult.

I was very, very lonely.

On that first night in the woods, the first night without Bone at my side, I slept fitfully in the leaf nest. I was afraid to fall too soundly asleep. In our shed I had felt safe, protected from the likes of Mine or coyotes. But here in the woods I was exposed, and I didn't know what kinds of animals might be about. A strange dog had once wandered onto the Merrions' property, and Mother hadn't trusted it any more than she had trusted Mine. I remembered the growling thing at the garbage cans. What had that been? A dog?

But the night passed quietly and in the morning I explored my woods. They were small, but big enough so that I could retreat from the sight of the traffic and the mall. I found a stream with clear water in it. And on the other side of the woods, a good walk from the side that bordered the busy road, I discovered houses – set close together like the ones where George and Marcy lived. The woods faced the backs of the houses, and behind many of them were...garbage pails. Raiding them might be difficult, but I was glad to know they were there. I could reach them without crossing a busy road.

On that first day I nosed around the woods enough to gain an understanding of this new neighbourhood. It was similar to the forest neighbourhood at the edge of the Merrions' property. I discovered squirrels, chipmunks, groundhogs, skunks and many small rodents. I saw owls' nests and crows' nests and heard hawks and jays and chickadees and cardinals and sparrows and swallows. I saw several does, three large fawns who hadn't lost their spots yet, and a mother turkey and her half-grown chicks. I didn't see any cats, though, and found myself wishing for Yellow Man. I also didn't see any animals that might prey on me. If these woods were to be my home, they weren't bad. I missed Bone, but I felt fairly safe now and I could find food and water.

So I began my new life. I made a more protected den in the shelter of two large fir trees whose trunks grew so close together that they might have been a single tree, and whose branches spread wide and low, and shielded me from rain as the shed roof had done. Every morning I hunted. I drank from the stream and from puddles. Occasionally I made trips to the garbage cans behind the humans' houses. If I was lucky, a lid might be left off. Once, I saw a large dog digging through an overturned can. I waited until he left, then ate the scraps he didn't want.

The change in the weather happened so slowly that at first I didn't notice it. Then late one afternoon as the sun slunk out of the sky I realized how chilly the air was. I looked above me at the leafy canopy and saw that it was now many hues, instead of the one humans would call green. And I could see more sky than before. The nights seemed to have grown longer and the days shorter. Sometimes my breath turned to mist in the air.

One morning I took a walk to a large puddle that had formed during a rainstorm and found that overnight it had become hard. I didn't know what ice was, and I licked at it. It was cold. And to my surprise, slippery. I couldn't drink from it, and I was relieved to discover that the stream was still running, although the water in it was frigid.

Time passed and soon there were no leaves at all on the trees. The branches of the pines that sheltered my den were dense and sweeping, but the branches of the other trees lay stark against the sky, like the skeleton of a fawn I had once found in the woods near the Merrions' house. On the day snow began to fall I first watched in amazement, then ran into the flakes to play. Bone would have loved the snow, and I wished I could have played in it with him instead of alone. Still...I ran, I pounced, I leaped. It was only later that I discovered how difficult hunting and finding food became in the snow. And exactly how cold my outdoor bed could be.

But I survived the winter, my first winter, and was just as surprised to feel the air warm and to see the leaves return as I had been to feel the air cool and to watch the leaves fall. The snow melted, and the ice at the edges of the stream broke away and was carried off in the currents and rivulets. A young doe gave birth to two fawns. The birds built nests and laid eggs. It was a time of sunlight and babies and newness and rich smells from the damp earth.

I was hungry, though. I was lean after the long winter, I was still growing, and lately I hadn't had much luck hunting. There came a time when I had caught nothing in two days. I began prowling around behind the houses, eyeing the garbage cans, but once a man had run outside, yelling at me and waving his arms. And twice I had seen the big dog, so I had retreated quietly into the shadows of the woods.

On the evening of the fourth day with no food, an evening when the air was particularly warm, I ventured to the other side of my woods. I hadn't been to the mall since the day Bone and I were thrown away there, but at certain times, and when the wind blew in a certain direction, I could smell the garbage from the cans there. The busy road lay between me and all that garbage, but I didn't care. I was so hungry that my insides felt as though they were shrivelling up. If I waited until full dark maybe I could have one good meal from the garbage, then return to my woods and try hunting again.

I stood by the side of the road, watching the cars with their bright eyes stream by. *WHOOSH-WHOOSH-WHOOSH.*

My stomach growled.

I turned and watched the road in one direction for a while. No eyes were coming. I looked in the other direction, and that was when I noticed another dog, also standing at the edge of the road watching the eyes, concentrating on the traffic. I was about to turn and run when I saw that the dog was the same shade of colour as Bone, had Bone's face, was Bone grown up, although he was smaller than me, his proud tail – now fat and fluffy – held high in the air.

I crept towards him, then let out a yip of joy.

At my yip, the dog turned quickly, but didn't bark, just watched my approach. And I could tell, from several feet away, that this wasn't Bone at all. This dog was a female.

I jumped back. I let out a growl and my lip curled into a snarl. But the small dog wagged her tail at me and put her rump in the air, chest and front legs on the ground. Then she dropped her rump and crawled towards me on her belly.

I approached her again slowly. I sniffed at her snout, and my own tail began to wag.

My new friend was named Moon, and she did look very much like Bone, or at least the way Bone might look now that he was grown. Moon and I never did cross the road that night. Instead, feeling braver with a companion at my side, I led Moon through the woods to the row of houses and we raided the garbage cans there after all. It was a gloomy, overcast night, and by now it was very late, so not many lights were on at the houses. We crept across the yard of the darkest house to find two cans with loose lids.

After a huge feast of scraps and spoiled fruit, my stomach swollen with food, I returned to my den under the fir trees. Moon followed me. She followed me onto the leaf bed, too, and when I curled up, she curled around me, her snout and front paws resting on my back. We slept that way all night, and I dreamed of Mother and Bone and the wheelbarrow.

I awoke the next day as the sky lightened and the birds began their morning songs. Moon was still on the leaf bed, now stretched out on her stomach, head resting on her front paws.

When I saw this, I knew she was there to stay.

On the Move

Moon may have been little, but she was brave – brave and bold and adventurous like Bone. Once she knew where the garbage cans were, she visited them regularly. She was more inclined to raid the garbage than to hunt. On our first morning together I left our den and began poking around in the undergrowth for small animals. I expected Moon to join me, but tail held high, she headed in the direction of the houses. She looked at me over her shoulder several times, so after a moment I took my nose out of the undergrowth, even though I was positive I could smell a mouse in there, and I followed her.

At the edge of the woods I sat on my haunches and surveyed the backs of the houses as I usually did before approaching the garbage cans.

Not Moon. She marched boldly across one of the yards, reminding me of Mine, not bothering to listen for voices or to look around for other dogs. She had just reached the nearest can and I was wondering what she was going to do, since the lid looked fastened securely and Moon wasn't big enough to knock it over, when – *BANG*.

At the back of the house a door had opened, then slammed shut, and a woman carrying two large bags of garbage high-stepped across the wet grass in her bedroom slippers. She stopped suddenly when she saw Moon and dropped the bags onto the lawn. "Hey, doggie," she said. "What are you doing here? Who do you belong to?"

Moon was gone in a flash. She zipped towards the woods and as she did, I retreated, not wanting to be seen by the woman. I was ready to return to my hunting – to the undergrowth, and the mouse I knew was in there. But after a moment, I realized Moon wasn't behind me, so I turned and stole back to the edge of the woods.

There was Moon, sitting beneath a tree, watching the woman who was watching her. As soon as the woman had put the bags in the pails and disappeared inside her house, Moon ventured out of the woods again, but this time she went to the house next door. I could see two garbage cans there, each with its lid on. Moon paused between them and looked up. She stood on her hind legs and placed her front paws against one of the cans. Then she nosed the lid with her snout, and with a clatter the lid fell to the pavement.

I had been sitting on my haunches, but now I leaped onto all four feet. I was ready to turn and run into the woods again, but instead found myself running towards Moon. When I reached the garbage can, I pulled it over easily, and Moon and I surveyed the bounty. Someone had thrown away half a ham. We pounced and were devouring it noisily when I heard a voice say, "There it is! Oh, look. There are two dogs now."

I yelped, then jumped backwards, growling.

Behind me were two women, one of them from the house next door. "The little one is the one I saw before," she was saying. "I don't know where the big one came from."

"What should we do?" asked the other woman. "Call the pound?"

"I suppose so."

But Moon and I were halfway back to the woods by then. And when we did reach the woods, I saw that Moon was carrying the rest of the ham in her mouth.

After that, Moon checked the garbage cans frequently, but she never again found anything as wonderful as the ham. And we discovered that the lids on the cans were now apt to be fastened extra tightly, and that some people began placing bricks on the lids.

I returned to my hunting and had good luck again. Moon, though, was not a talented hunter. I shared my kills with her, but hunting for two was much more work than hunting just for myself, and Moon and I were often hungry. One day I noticed Moon sitting at the edge of the busy road, watching the traffic and the mall beyond. I thought of Bone waking at night in our shed and listening to the coyotes in the hills, and I wasn't surprised when on the next day Moon emerged from our den and began walking through the woods, not towards the mall, not towards the houses, but along the creek bed in the direction of the rising sun. I knew she wasn't going to come back.

So I left the den, too. I felt little attachment to it, wanted only the company of Moon. This was different from following Bone, though. When I was a puppy I had followed Bone away from our home because I was frightened. Now I was following Moon because I was brave. I had lived on my own for a long time, I had done lots of things on my own – scary things, things I did not want to do. I knew I could be Squirrel Alone. But I didn't have to be. So I bravely left the woods, my home for many changes of the moon, and followed my new friend.

On that first day we walked until the woods ended and the creek emptied into a small pond. Beyond the pond stood a house. Not far beyond that house was another. And another and another. These houses were smaller than the Merrions' but larger than Marcy and George's, and they were set far apart, surrounded by gardens, large trees and woods. The morning had dawned sunny with a clear blue sky, but as Moon and I had travelled along the creek bed, the day had darkened and the air had grown first damp, then misty. Now as Moon and I sat looking at the house by the pond, the fog drifted around us like smoke, hiding trees and bits of the house, then revealing them again, so that for a while I saw the yard only in pieces.

It was early summer. The leaves on the trees were still new, and until this morning the air had been warm, even hot. But now Moon and I were chilly. I stood up and shook myself off. I was hungry, but more than anything, I wanted to be warm and dry. Through the blowing fog I thought I could see a shed. It stood across the pond from the house. I trotted towards it, Moon at my heels.

We found the shed, but no way into it. It was sturdily built and the door was closed tightly.

Moon and I, shivering now, skirted the edges of the yard, tromped through a garden, and found another shed. No way in.

Just as the air became so heavy with moisture that the mist turned into a driving rain, I spotted a large structure. I know now that it was a barn, but I didn't know what it was then. The barn was dark; no lighted windows like we saw in the houses. And there were several open doors. Moon and I ran towards the barn, the rain biting into our skin. I came to a fast stop at one of the open doors.

So many odours with so much to tell me. Moon and I stood still, our noses in the air. I smelled grain, I smelled mice, I smelled cats, I smelled hay. I smelled people, but only faintly. What I smelled most strongly was an animal odour I couldn't quite identify. It turned out to be horses, which I had seen once or twice on the road near the Merrions' house.

Moon and I crept into the barn and nosed around until we found a warm, dry spot near a door in case we had to leave quickly. We settled as far from the other barn animals as we could get, and spent the night there. When we awoke in the morning, the sun had returned and the air was warm again. Moon and I scrounged for food, then went on our way.

Moon and I travelled together for many days, following streams or roads, but making sure to stay well away from the roads so that people in cars couldn't see us. We walked through woods and pastures. When we came to a town or a farm, we looked for food and for dry places in which to sleep. Sometimes we stayed in one spot for several days, but mostly we were on the move, trotting along shoulder to shoulder, my friend Moon and I.

The Fight

It was full summer when Moon and I came to the resting place near the highway. The days were still long but beginning to grow shorter, the leaves had a dusty grey look to them, and the crickets and katydids and other noisy insects made such a racket that sometimes at night I had trouble listening for predators.

Moon and I had travelled for hours that day, walking through the woods, keeping a highway to one side of us. We were tired, we were hungry, we had burrs in our ears and tails, and Moon had stepped on a sharp stick and her paw was bleeding.

Moon was sitting near a fallen log, licking her wound, when I caught the first whiff of garbage. I had been resting beside Moon, was dozing in the shade with my eyes half closed, when the odour reached my nose. I jumped to my feet and breathed in deeply. I was tempted to run towards that good smell, but I moved slowly because I could also smell humans.

Moon gave her foot a final lick and followed me. I stalked through the woods until I came to a clearing. I could hear traffic nearby, but I couldn't see the highway. In the clearing were several wooden tables with benches, a building in which humans could go to the toilet, and lots of garbage cans. Nearby was a stretch of asphalt like the one at the mall. Several cars were parked on it. I had been to places like this before and had seen cars pull off the highway and park on the asphalt. Then people would climb out of the cars, sit down at the tables, and eat food that they would remove from bags and boxes. They would eat and talk and stretch, and that was how I knew this was a highway resting place.

I looked at the tables and benches now and saw only two people sitting and eating. Moon and I watched them and after a few minutes, they stood, gathered up papers and bags and cans from their table, dumped the things in the nearest garbage can, and returned to their car. As soon as the car had driven away, Moon and I trotted into the resting place.

We ran to the first garbage can we saw and I pushed it over. Moon crawled inside and began pawing the contents onto the grass. Picnic leftovers, Moon and I had learned, could be very, very good. Here we found apple cores, the ends of sandwiches, nearly empty potato-chip bags, pieces of devilled eggs, cookie crumbs and a whole slice of cheese.

I pounced on the cheese, and Moon grabbed the end of a sandwich. We ate and ate, pausing from time to time to listen to the traffic, listen for the sound of an approaching car.

We heard nothing until the growling started.

Moon was inside the garbage can again then, rummaging through the papers, and I was at the mouth of the can, eating a pretzel. When we heard the first growl, Moon shot out of the can and ran into me, and I dropped the pretzel and turned around, my hackles raised.

It was twilight, that time of day when shadows grow long and the light starts to fade and a dog's eyes can play tricks on her. I looked in the direction of the growling, but at first I could see only the humans' toilet, and beyond that, the edge of the woods through which Moon and I had been travelling. A moment later, I thought I saw movement, but I wasn't sure.

The growling deepened.

And then I saw the eyes in the woods. A street light had turned itself on, and its rays made the eyes glow. I saw so many pairs of eyes that my body jerked and I began to pant. I looked around at Moon and in that instant a pack of dogs rushed out of the twilight, teeth bared, snarling and yipping.

Moon and I broke into a run and streaked away from the dogs. We ran and ran, not caring where we were headed or whether any people saw us. I ran faster than I had ever run. I ran so that my ears blew back from my head. I ran so that I could barely feel the ground under my paws. I ran until my chest heaved and my breath came heavy and fast. Twice I glanced over my shoulder to make sure Moon was keeping up with me. When I saw her at my heels I ran even faster.

The dogs were following us, I was sure of that. But Moon and I were faster than they were. We ran and ran and ran and ran until...*WHOOSH-WHOOSH-WHOOSH*. Suddenly the highway spread before us, cars speeding by in both directions. I stopped short and once again Moon crashed into me. We had almost darted onto the highway, darted among all those cars and trucks, into that blur of metal and tyres.

We backed away, turned around, and started running again. Night was falling. I wasn't sure where the resting place was. I smelled food, but it seemed too nearby to come from the garbage cans we'd been eating from. So I led Moon towards the good smells, and the next thing I knew the dogs – the same vicious dogs – were all around us. We were back in the resting place after all.

The dogs were starving. They were desperate. And there were lots of them. The moment they spotted Moon and me they charged towards us. We couldn't run away; they formed a circle around us. For one moment, before the fight began, the scene seemed frozen like the puddle in the woods, and I could see every dog clearly. They were different shapes and sizes, but all stood stiffly, ears back, snarling and bristling. I could see their ribs, their entire skeletons, forming knobby ridges under their skin. Their fur was patchy and dirty. One dog seemed to have almost no fur at all. And their eyes were rheumy and runny.

I edged closer to Moon, close enough to feel her body heat. Moon was panting heavily, her own legs stiff, her own ears back, a snarl escaping from her mouth.

Moon was the littlest dog there.

I noticed all this, as if the world had stopped, and then everything jerked back into motion. The dogs ran at us, snapping. I bared my teeth. When one of the dogs leaped on me, we rolled around and around on the asphalt, fangs bared. I snarled and yipped and sank my teeth into the dog's flank. I felt her teeth sink into my neck.

Two dogs slammed into Moon, throwing her to the ground. They jumped on her, and the three of them became a whirl of fur and teeth and claws. I heard Moon scream, but then one of her attackers let out a scream of his own and leaped away. He sank to the ground and lay there, panting hard. The other dog also backed away, and when Moon stalked towards him, he turned and limped behind a trash can.

The dog who had bitten my neck now stood before me, poised to charge again. But I surprised her. I charged first, grabbing her bony shoulder between my jaws. The dog shrieked, pulled herself from my grasp, and ran off. I looked around for Moon and felt a blow on my back. The biggest of the dogs had jumped on me first. Our heads knocked together, my tooth pierced my lip, my skull smashed onto the asphalt. I was at the bottom of a heap of flesh and limbs. I was smothering. I couldn't see.

And then the dogs began to roll off me and slink away. Moon was at my side, still snarling, still baring her teeth, still menacing the other dogs. Our attackers were old and weak and unhealthy, but they had made their point. They kept their eyes trained on Moon and me. When we began to edge out of the resting area, out of their territory, they turned towards the trash cans.

Moon and I moved as fast as we could, but I didn't have the strength to run. We limped along, keeping the resting place at our backs, the highway to one side, the woods to the other, as far from the traffic as possible. Soon, though, I felt as if I couldn't take another step. I sat down in the stubby grass.

Moon nudged me with her nose. I didn't budge. Moon nudged me again and turned into the woods. After a moment I followed her. She picked her way through the undergrowth and flopped down on a little bed of leaves.

I thought the bed might have belonged to a deer, but I didn't care. I flopped down, too.

I was still breathing heavily, and every part of my body hurt. I licked at Moon, searching for her injuries, and she licked at me. We were bleeding from many cuts and scratches. I found several bites on Moon, but none seemed too deep. One of Moon's ears was torn, though, and one of my front paws had a gash in it. Moon found the gash and licked away.

After a while Moon began to lick her own wounds and I licked mine. I licked and licked and licked and licked. When the taste of blood faded, I laid my head on my front paws and rested. Presently Moon stopped licking, too, and she curled up on her side, her back to my chest.

We fell into a deep sleep on our leaf bed in the strange woods, our bodies aching, our heads throbbing, our mouths dry. Overhead, the moon rose and circled the sky. Crickets chirped, owls hunted and hooted. I think the deer returned in search of her bed. She watched us for some time, then left quietly.

Moon and I slept on.

Healing

That night I licked my wounds as I slept. I licked and slept, licked and dreamed. I was in exquisite pain.

The dreams circled around me. My bruised body floated above the ground, and below, far below, I saw the vicious dogs and my old den in the woods and the mall and Marcy and George's house, and then I was above the Merrions' house, swallows swooping by the chimneys and roofs. I could feel the whisper of their wings against my fur.

On the lawn, which seemed a very long way down, I saw Matthias reading in the shade of a tree. The other boy and the noisy girl were spraying each other with the garden hose, shrieking and laughing. They sprayed Matthias and he jumped to his feet, the book falling out of his lap. Then, like a snake, he glided across the grass and slid under our shed.

The sky and the swallows and the rooftops disappeared suddenly, and I found myself among the rafters in the shed, still looking down, watching what was below. And there was my family. Mother and Bone and I were sleeping in the wheelbarrow. We breathed steadily and heavily. Bone's foot twitched as he dreamed, as I dreamed of his dreams. A mouse emerged from a small hole near a roof beam, scampered to a spot just above Mother's head, and watched us solemnly. Mother stirred, Bone stirred, I stirred. The mouse crept away and we slept on.

I felt myself falling then, crashing, and I awoke with a jerk that made my body throb. Next to me Moon quivered, rolled over, and licked at a bite on her rear leg. When I drifted into sleep again, I found myself back at the shed, but this time Mother was gone and Bone and I were sitting on the burlap nest. Matthias eased quietly through the door and held out his hand to us. When he opened it, a swallow was perched on his palm. Matthias set the swallow on the floor and left the shed. The swallow flew up into the rafters, and when I turned to look at it, I found myself outside, hunting with Bone in the woods. I was hungry. My stomach was rumbling. Bone and I couldn't find the garbage heap. I was thirsty, too, my mouth as dry as sand.

I woke and saw that Moon was gone. I was alone on the leaf bed. I licked my feet and fell asleep again. I slept and dreamed and woke and licked. Sometimes when I awoke, Moon was next to me; sometimes the leaf bed was empty. Sometimes the light in the woods was bright, the sun shining through the leaves; sometimes the woods were in darkness except for weak moonlight. I slept for a day and a night and another day and another night and part of the day after that. Moon stayed close by. When she left the leaf bed, she didn't go far.

On the day after the second night, I awoke from a dream about finding cake with white frosting in the garbage heap, and I realized that my aching body didn't ache quite so much. I rose, gingerly putting weight on my sore feet. Moon had been dozing beside me, but now she jumped to her feet. She touched my nose with hers, then licked my snout. I licked at her ear, at the scabby notch that had formed after the dogs tore it.

Then I stepped off the leaf bed. As in my dreams, my stomach was empty and growling, and my mouth dry and sandy. I staggered a bit. I didn't feel up to hunting for food, but I didn't know if any garbage cans were nearby. And how far away was a stream or a puddle?

I was about to sink back on the leaf bed when Moon nudged me, then headed purposefully into the woods, keeping her back to the highway. She led me to the edge of a small brook. I stood on its banks and drank and drank. Then I waded into the water and let it wash over my bruised feet. I remembered chasing Bone through the stream on the day we left the Merrions' property. That was when we were puppies, healthy puppies. Now my feet felt as heavy as logs. I couldn't imagine running and chasing and playing.

I picked my way over the stones in the brook and up the bank where I sat down next to Moon. Moon looked at me, then jerked to attention and cocked her head. In an instant she had leaped away and buried her head in a patch of tall grass. She emerged with a fat vole, which she laid at my feet. Then she dived into the grass again and emerged with a second vole. Moon, who preferred not to hunt, had caught a meal for me.

I was healing. With Moon at my side, little Moon with her notched ear, my strength returned, my bruises disappeared, and soon all that was left of my cuts and bites were small bare patches in my fur.

Moon and I stayed in the woods until one morning we awoke and knew that we were going to leave our leaf bed. We set off through the woods, keeping the highway to one side.

Moon and I were on the move again.

Town Dogs

Moon and I travelled as another summer came to an end. We loped through yards where chrysanthemums and autumn crocuses bloomed. We ran through fields where the tall grasses had become brittle and rattled in the wind. We wandered through woods as the leaves on the trees grew dry and changed colour and fell down on us, swirling about our feet. The air turned cold, and before I knew it we needed to find shelters that would keep us warm, as well as protect us.

I don't know how far we travelled, only that we walked and walked and walked and walked. Moon's ear, permanently notched, lost its scab, and some of the fur grew back. My fur grew back, too, covering all the scars except for a long curved one on my front paw. No fur ever grew there again, and I was reminded of the starving, desperate dogs every time I looked at my foot.

One dark, damp day, the leaves still clinging to the trees, Moon and I were trotting through a farmer's field when something wet and cold landed on my snout. I was trying to reach it with my tongue when I felt an icy tickle on my ear, then on my back. I looked at Moon and saw tiny crystals in her fur.

Snow.

The first snow had come early, the trees not yet bare, late flowers still in bloom. It melted quickly, but the next night more snow fell.

Several evenings later Moon and I found ourselves at the edge of a small town. We stood just inside some bushy undergrowth and looked out at a street lined with houses like Marcy and George's. We were hungry, but we made no move to find food. Something strange was happening. Even though darkness had fallen, lots of children were roaming the street. They were carrying bags, and they were not dressed like any children I had ever seen. Some of them wore paint on their faces. Some wore clothing that glittered. Some wore large hats. I peered hard through the trees and realized that one child was dressed to look like a reptile, and another resembled a cat. I saw a dog, too, and even an ice-cream cone.

The children laughed and shouted and called to one another. Small groups of them would stand at the doors of the houses and shout, "Trick or treat!" Then the doors would open and people in the houses would toss things into the children's bags.

Moon and I were still watching from the woods when once again I felt icy crystals on my snout.

"Snowing! It's snowing!" the children cried. They continued to run up and down the street with their bags, but now they danced through the little white eddies whirling around their feet, and tipped their heads back to catch snowflakes on their tongues.

Moon and I waited a long time in the woods that night. When the last child had left the street, and the lights in the houses had winked out, we slunk out of our hiding place. We nosed our way up and down the street. We found lots of food that the children had dropped, but we didn't eat much of it. It was all very sweet, and I had learned in the past that although chocolate tasted good, I didn't feel well after I ate it.

The next day we left the town. We roamed through woods for many days, and the early snow kept falling. The moon grew large and full, then became a thin slice of light in the frosty sky. One day I was watching Moon sleep behind an abandoned shed, and I realized I could see her ribs. Hunting had been difficult in the unexpected snow and we hadn't had much luck with garbage lately. But I was startled to look at Moon and see in her place one of the bony dogs from the resting place. How long until my friend would be as desperate as they were?

Moon was tired. She wasn't able to walk as far each day as we had walked during the summer. I nudged her now, wanting her to get to her feet, and she gave a small growl and turned her back on me. I allowed Moon to rest for one day, then I left the shed in the woods, knowing she would follow me.

And she did.

We were off again, and this time I let my nose lead us. I was sniffing for the scents of a town. My nose took us first to a road – a busy road, but not a highway. Moon and I followed it, trying to stay out of sight of cars, until, from the top of a low hill, I could see a town in a valley – rooftops and treetops and church spires. We left the road then, and walked down the hill, through woods and fields, keeping the town in front of us. We stopped for food from the garbage cans at a gas station, then continued towards the town.

It was late afternoon, the sun setting over the hill, sending its last rays through the chilly air, when Moon and I reached a point just outside the town. We paused in a field and I looked down, surveying this place that might become our home for the winter.

The town – eventually I learned that it was called Claremont – did become our home that winter. Claremont consisted of a single main road called Nassau Street that was lined with businesses, restaurants and small shops. Several side streets crossed Nassau. The houses on these streets backed up to woods and hills. At each end of the town stood a long, low building. After a time Moon and I discovered that one building was a supermarket and the other was a school. There was great garbage at each place.

As far as I could see, this town was a good spot for dogs in winter. Moon and I would be able to find plenty of food.

The garbage cans filled up quickly, and we could also go hunting if necessary. And there were lots of shelters – old sheds and storage rooms and garages that weren't used at night, as well as the woods if we didn't want to be quite so close to humans.

I liked living in Claremont. I had never considered myself a town dog, but in this cold, snowy winter it was a fine place to settle down. Moon and I spent a lot of time watching Nassau Street from hiding places. Sometimes we were watching for danger, sometimes we were watching for food, sometimes we were just watching.

There was a rhythm to life in Claremont. On most mornings after Moon and I foraged for our breakfast, we would skirt around the houses on the side streets until we reached a stand of trees on Nassau between a shop that sold books and a shop that sold jewellery. We would settle in the undergrowth there and watch the town come to life. A man named Robert owned the jewellery store. A woman named Lisa owned the bookstore. Each morning they greeted each other as they met on the street. "Morning, Robert!" "Morning, Lisa!" Then they bought coffee at a bakery, brought the coffee to their stores, and unlocked the doors.

Up and down the street other workers arrived and other stores and businesses opened – the shoe store, the toy store, the stationery store, the sandwich shop, the restaurants, the movie theatre, the library and a few places that were mysteries to Moon and me. We could see people inside these places sitting at desks, using pens, looking at blinking screens. Men and women from the street entered these places, and talked to the people at the desks, and passed papers back and forth, and left. Not nearly as interesting as the toy store, or better yet, the restaurants.

One store was of particular interest to Moon and me. It was named The Wagging Tail, but Robert called it the pet shop. Moon and I investigated it as thoroughly as we could by sniffing around both its front and back doors at night when Nassau Street was deserted. The Wagging Tail didn't sell any actual pets, but it sold all sorts of things for animals. It sold food for dogs and cats and birds and fish and guinea pigs. It sold things for these animals to play with, like the things Matthias brought to Bone and me in the shed. It even sold outfits for dogs. Once, on a rainy day, I saw a small, curly-haired white dog enter the store with his owner and come out wearing a yellow raincoat to keep him dry. Moon and I watched, shivering from our spot under the drippy bushes, as the dog walked down the street in his new coat, eating a biscuit.

In the middle of the day when the sun was the highest, the people of Claremont would have their lunch. Shoppers would duck into the bakery or one of the restaurants before continuing with their errands. Robert always walked to the sandwich shop, bought chicken salad on rye, a cup of split pea soup, and another cup of coffee, and carried the things back to the jewellery store, where he ate behind the counter. He almost never finished his lunch, and we soon learned to look for the remains of the chicken salad sandwich when he took his trash outside at the end of the day.

Later in the afternoon, school would finish, and some of the older children would run along Nassau Street, stopping in at the candy store or the bakery or the bookstore. Two girls, Amanda and Sarah, whose mother, Moon and I learned, worked in the library, always left school and walked to the library, but first they would stop at the toy store and gaze at the things in its windows. They never went inside, just stopped and looked.

When the day began to grow dark, the stores in Claremont would close up. One by one Robert and Lisa and the other shop owners turned out their lights, locked their doors, and got in their cars or walked down the street to their homes. Much later, when the town was quiet and almost as dark as the night, Moon and I foraged for food. Sometimes we would see other dogs looking for food, but we stayed away from them. These dogs were skinny and tired, not fat and bouncy like the little white dog in the raincoat, but they didn't bother Moon and me and we didn't bother them. Up and down the street Moon and I would walk, checking garbage cans, sniffing in corners. We walked from the grocery store at one end of town to the school at the other. We usually found enough food to fill our stomachs. And then we would look for a place where we could settle down for the night, and sleep safely and warmly.

When Moon and I first arrived in Claremont I noticed that fastened to many of the doors in town were bunches of corncobs, or wreaths of dried chrysanthemums. But one day, after we had been in Claremont for some time – long enough to learn the names of Robert and Lisa and Amanda and Sarah and to know the rhythms of the town – I noticed a change. The corn and the chrysanthemums were taken down and in their place were hung wreaths of evergreens with big bows and shiny bells. Robert spent a morning putting ropes of pine boughs around the window of his shop. Lisa strung lights in the window of the bookstore. And in the very centre of Claremont the tall fir tree that stood between the library and the post office was also strung with lights. Moon and I saw more people than usual shopping in town, hurrying along, cheerfully carrying bags and bundles, looking busy but happy.

Sarah and Amanda continued to peer into the toy store after school, and one day they finally went inside. When they came out, each was carrying a small bag, and they chattered and skipped and Amanda sang, "You better watch out, you better not cry!"

Sarah grinned. "You didn't peek, did you?"

"Nope," said Amanda. "Did you?"

"Nope."

"I have enough left over to get something for Mom, I think."

"Me, too."

"Let's go to the chemist's tomorrow and look at the perfume."

* * *

A few days later the shoppers were still eating their lunches and having their morning coffee when the doors to the school opened and the children spilled out into the street.

"School's over!" they shouted.

"Three more days until Christmas!" cried two boys.

Amanda and Sarah ran down Nassau Street, blue scarves flying, and instead of stopping at the toy store, they stopped at the bakery and emerged from it carrying cookies shaped like people.

Two days after that, when the afternoon was growing dark and it was time for the stores to close, something new happened. People began to stream into Claremont from every direction. Moon and I, pressed close together in our hiding place, drew back, afraid we might be discovered. But everyone was looking at the street. People lined it on both sides.

"Merry Christmas!" they called.

"Happy holidays!"

Sarah and Amanda hurried along later, holding their mother's hands.

"Did we miss him?" asked Sarah. "We didn't miss him, did we?"

"The parade hasn't even started, silly," said Amanda.

"Yes, it has! Yes, it has!" shrieked Sarah. "There it is!"

The people, who had been cheering, now became quiet, and Moon and I tried to see what was happening. Down Nassau Street, shining in the darkness, came a group of people singing songs, and then some people riding on funny cars, throwing things to the children on the sidewalk. And then...

"I see him!" cried Sarah. "There's Santa Claus!"

Moon and I couldn't see Santa Claus, whoever he was. The people lining the street had crowded together even more tightly. We saw legs, lots of legs. And we heard the cheering start again. The people cheered and cheered, and then the parade ended and the crowd began to drift out of town.

When everyone had gone home, Moon and I ventured onto Nassau Street. Claremont was quiet now, nearly silent. We sniffed along the sidewalks for a few minutes, and found a mitten, two hats and some very strong-smelling striped candies, which we licked at. The parade had made me nervous, but in the sudden quiet, I found that I felt brave again. So I touched Moon's nose with mine, and we set off in search of garbage.

The Long Winter

After Moon and I had scrounged for supper – the rest of Robert's sandwich plus a split bag of something crunchy that we found outside the back door of The Wagging Tail – we returned to Nassau Street. Never before had we walked directly down the main street of Claremont, not during the day and not during the night. But not a single person was about, so we felt more free than usual. Most of the store windows were still lit up, and as we passed them we could see silent figures dressed in bright colours, and sparkly decorations, and toys and candy and ribbons.

When we reached the corner where the bakery stood,

we turned down a side street called Tinker Lane. The windows of most of the houses here were lit, too, but we felt brave enough on this quiet, quiet night to pause in the front yards and try to see what was happening inside the houses. Moon and I had not peeked in many windows during our lives, but we had peeked in a few, and this was the first time we had ever seen fir trees in people's homes. They were smaller than the one on Nassau Street, but they were strung with lights like the big tree and also hung with glittery decorations. We could see people standing by some of the trees and they were smiling or laughing. In one house we saw a little girl jumping up and down. In another we saw a boy tying a ribbon around the neck of a fuzzy black dog.

Moon and I wandered the streets until most of the lights had winked out. Then we spent the night huddled in the little space between two closed dumpsters in the parking lot at the supermarket.

It snowed during the night. Not much, though; just enough to add a clean layer to the snow that had already fallen. Only a few flakes drifted down onto Moon and me in our hideaway, and we awoke the next morning feeling warm and mostly dry.

We were just creeping out into the parking lot, looking around for signs of people or other dogs, when we heard the talking of humans and ducked back between the dumpsters.

"They're here every single morning," a woman's voice was saying.

"How many are there, do you think?" asked another voice, a man's.

"It varies," said the woman. "They're not a pack. Sometimes only a couple are here. Sometimes five or six. They're pretty wary of one another, but they're always here."

"Well, this is a nice thing you're doing. A Christmas present for the stray dogs."

I didn't hear anything else for a moment or two, so I stuck my snout out from between the dumpsters and looked in the direction of the voices. There they were, the woman and the man. The woman was very tall and the man was very short. They were dressed in warm clothes – scarves and mittens and big coats and knitted hats – and they were spooning something into aluminium pie tins.

Hamburger.

My nose told me that right away.

"It's not their fault they're strays," said the woman. "They shouldn't have to eat garbage all the time." She paused. "Some of them are practically starving."

Moon and I waited and watched. When the woman had finished spooning the hamburger into the pie tins, she and the man placed the tins around the parking lot. Then they climbed into a car and drove away.

The second the car was out of sight, Moon and I made a dash for the nearest tin. From out of other hiding places rushed three more dogs. In moments all the food was gone and the other dogs had disappeared.

The sun came out, and Moon and I basked in it, our stomachs full.

We spent that night – I know now that it was Christmas night – in the spot between the dumpsters. The next morning we were awakened earlier than usual by the sound of voices. The tall woman was back. This time she was with another woman, a woman with the longest hair I had ever seen.

"Look," I heard the tall woman say. "All the tins are empty."

"Licked clean."

"Let's get them filled up. We have to hurry. I want to do this before the store opens. I don't think the dogs will come out for food if anyone is around."

"And also," said the woman with the long hair, "we'd better do this without being seen."

The women worked quickly. They walked around the parking lot, filling each tin with more hamburger. When they were finished, they climbed into a car. But I noticed that this time they drove to the edge of the lot and stopped. Moon and I waited for a moment. The car didn't move. But two big dogs rushed for the pie tins, anyway, so Moon and I did the same. Before we were done, two more dogs arrived.

In no time the plates were empty. The women left then.

They were back the next day.

"I brought extra plates," said the tall woman. "And more hamburger. I didn't realize how quickly the dogs would eat everything."

"Maybe we should feed them twice a day," said the woman with the long hair.

"That's a good idea. We'll have to switch to dog food, though. We can't afford to keep buying meat."

"They can't live on hamburger alone anyway. They need more vitamins."

That was how Moon and I got lucky, at least for a while. The women and their friends visited the parking lot of the supermarket every morning before the store opened and every evening after it closed, leaving out plates of wet and dry food for the dogs who had made their homes in Claremont.

Moon and I continued to steer clear of the other dogs. They were nearby, of course. We passed them everywhere, and we all vied for the same food in town – whatever the garbage cans or pie tins had to offer. But I never forgot about the encounter with the dogs at the rest stop and trusted no dog except Moon.

The winter, that winter in Claremont, might have been cold and snowy, but for once, Moon and I didn't have any trouble finding food. Every morning we breakfasted at the parking lot. Then we would wander discreetly through Claremont, watching Robert and Lisa and Sarah and Amanda, watching as the Christmas decorations were taken down and in their place sprouted hearts and cupids, and later eggs and rabbits and chicks and baskets and candy. In the evening we would eat dinner at the parking lot again, then spend the night between the dumpsters.

We noticed that the other stray dogs now slept in the parking lot as well. And that there were more of them. By the time the air was growing warmer and crocuses and daffodils were starting to bloom in Claremont we noticed something else: occasionally a large, dark-coloured van was parked in the lot early in the morning. If it was there, the women wouldn't feed us. They would drive by the lot and not return until the van had left. Then they would feed us if the supermarket hadn't opened, but sometimes we missed our breakfast because of the van.

One morning, a bright warm morning with sniffs of spring in the air, the very tall woman and the woman with the long hair arrived at the parking lot, looked around for the van, then hurriedly filled the pie tins, placed them around the lot, and drove away. Moon and I and several other dogs had rushed to the tins and were beginning our breakfasts when the van eased into the lot and glided to a silent stop. I kept my eye on it as Moon and I bolted our food.

The front doors of the van opened quietly. Two men slipped out, each carrying a long pole with a loop of rope attached to one end. They pointed to the dogs eating from the pie tin nearest the van and ran towards them, poles extended. The dogs, a little one Moon's size and a bigger one, didn't see the men. In a flash, each man threw his loop around the neck of a dog and pulled tight.

Caught! The dogs were caught in the ropes. They yipped and barked and fought, jerking back and forth, pulling and snapping. But the men held tight to the poles and tugged the dogs towards the van. They threw open a door at the back and hauled the dogs into cages. Then they slammed the door shut. They stood in the lot, poles in hand.

"Do you see any of the others?" asked one of the men.

"Nope. They disappeared fast."

"They'll be back tomorrow. Or maybe tonight. Those people were feeding them at night, too, I think."

"All right. Well, let's get these two to the shelter. We'll come back here later."

That night after the supermarket had closed, Moon and I waited cautiously between our dumpsters. The women arrived, put out our food, and left. The moment they drove away, the van pulled into the parking lot. Moon and I ran into the woods and circled around to Nassau Street. We found supper behind The Wagging Tail and slept under the awning of the back entrance to Robert's jewellery store.

The next morning we made our way to the supermarket again. The van returned. It was time to leave Claremont.

On a windy day with clouds gathering on the horizon, Moon and I set off through the woods and left the town behind us.

Moon

Spring that year was long and slow and dry and warm. Moon and I had little trouble finding food. We were smarter now. Instead of avoiding towns we sought them out. But we were careful to linger mostly at the edges and not to stay too long. Whenever we arrived at a new town we explored it carefully. We studied its rhythms and looked for the pet stores and watched to see if anyone might be feeding stray dogs. We ate mostly in darkness, and we paid attention if we saw a van that was driving slowly. We stayed in each town for only a few days, then we lived in the woods for a time, keeping our hunting skills sharp, and then we moved on to another town.

In one town we slept behind a woodpile at a house where two women and two little girls lived. The women caught sight of us and set out dishes of food and water, and seemed very kind. Outside another town we discovered a small farm with a barn that housed a donkey named Tico and a cow named Bluebell. We slept in an empty stall for three nights, drinking water from a large tub and dining on birdseed, grain and little red squirrels. Then we moved on. As the moon changed from the tiny curl of a cat's claw to a half-closed eye, and the days grew longer and even warmer, my friend and I slept in towns, on farms, and once in an open field where the night-time sounds reminded me of an evening at the Merrions' when I had watched Mine trot through their yard.

One day, one of the longest of the year, when the sun rose early and set late, Moon and I left a town called Republic. We hadn't liked the town. As soon as we'd arrived we'd seen a man kick a dog that was tied up in a yard on a very short chain. Later, after we had discovered a feed store in town, we were waiting in some bushes for the store to close, when a group of boys and girls who were not little but were not grown-ups yet either, discovered our hiding place and threw rocks at us. One rock, with a sharp point on it, hit me behind my ear, and a large one landed square on Moon's back. We were on our way out of Republic, my head bleeding slightly, when we came upon a grocery store where a man was putting some cheese and stale bread and the ends of sausages in a bowl by the back door. He saw us as we were running away, paused, then added more sausage to the bowl before he went inside. So Moon and I waited until dark and ate our supper at the store. Then we spent the night at an abandoned gas station. But the next morning we left Republic behind us.

We had wakened early, checked the bowl at the grocery store, found it still licked clean from the night before, and set out. Very quickly we reached some woods. We trotted through them, our stomachs empty but not grumbling too loudly. We had just passed through a small clearing when we came to a sleepy mountain road and spotted two chipmunks perched on a fallen log on the other side.

Moon sprinted across the road and I was after her in a flash. We were so intent on surprising the chipmunks that neither of us heard the truck that came thundering around a bend in the road, not until it was almost upon us.

I looked up in time to see the terrible blue thing, like an enormous dog with big yellow eyes and a row of gleaming teeth, bearing down on us. I heard a person scream and the truck make a loud squeal, and I jumped backwards. Moon had already reached the middle of the road, though, and the truck hit her at high speed and sent her flying. It only clipped me, but it clipped the shoulder that had been injured when George had thrown Bone and me away, and I couldn't move, so I lay at the edge of the woods.

I yelped for Moon, but I didn't hear any sound from her.

The truck flew past, still squealing, and its tyres locked in place as it skidded down the road, leaving long marks that swerved from side to side and finally ended as the truck came to an abrupt stop.

I heard more screams and then the screams became voices, but I couldn't see who was speaking.

"A dog! You hit a dog!"

"No, *two* dogs. I think there were two."

"They came out of nowhere."

"It wasn't your fault."

"They just ran right in front of me."

"Is everyone okay?"

"I'm okay."

"I'm okay."

"Is the truck okay?"

"I think so."

A little silence followed, and I lifted my head to see where Moon was. She had landed by the log – the chipmunks had disappeared, of course – and she lay still. I dropped my head back to the ground.

I heard footsteps running in the road then, and soon I could see several pairs of legs. Two feet with sneakers on them stopped next to me. A girl who was about the age of Matthias Merrion's brother leaned over and peered into my face. She put out a hand and rested it on my back for a moment. "This one's alive. I think it's going to be okay," she said.

I watched some other sneakers cross the road. A woman stooped down beside Moon. She ran her hand down Moon's back and rolled her over gently. "This one's dead, I'm afraid, but let's take both of them to the vet."

"I'll bring the truck back here," said a man, and a third pair of sneakers walked down the road towards the truck.

The girl sat next to me at the edge of the woods and put her arms around me.

"Be careful!" the woman called to her. "I don't want you touching a strange dog."

"Well, it's not bleeding or anything," the girl replied.

I tried to figure out how many people had been in the truck. There was this girl, and the woman who was sitting with Moon, and the man who had gone for the truck, and now I realized there was a boy, too. He crossed the road and kneeled beside Moon and the woman.

I wanted to look at Moon again but my head had grown very heavy, and as the girl stroked my back I fell asleep. I woke up when I felt a pair of strong arms lift me from the ground. The arms belonged to the man and he set me carefully in the back of the truck. A moment later he laid Moon next to me and I could tell that she was indeed dead. I had seen many dead things in my life, and now Moon was one of them.

Part Three

Gentle Hands

I slept in the back of the truck until I felt it jerk to a stop. Then I heard doors slamming, and then, just like before, all the people began to talk at once.

"Here we are."

"I hope they're open. Is the vet open on Saturday, do you think?"

"I'll run inside."

"What do they do with dead dogs?"

"Hush. Don't worry about that now."

"Hello! We have an emergency here!" That was the man. He was calling to someone.

A few moments later the doors at the back of the truck were opened and first I and then Moon were slid out and rushed inside a building. A woman in blue clothing opened a door and hurried all of us – the man, the woman, the girl, the boy, Moon and me – into a small room where Moon and I were laid side by side on a table. The woman in blue was opening drawers and laying things on a counter, when another woman, this one wearing a white smock, bustled into the room.

She held out her hand to the man and the woman and said, "Hi, I'm Dr Roth. I understand we have an emergency." Before the man or the woman could answer her, Dr Roth began to examine Moon.

"We don't know whose dogs they are," said the man after a few moments, "or whether they even have owners." He shook his head. "We think that one is dead," he added, indicating Moon.

Dr Roth nodded. "I'm afraid so. If it makes you feel better, she probably died instantly. She didn't have time to feel any pain."

I heard the woman let out her breath. "Well, I guess that's good. We do feel terrible, though. Even if it was an accident. I mean, we never saw the dogs coming. We were driving down Bostock, and they just came flying out of the woods."

"They're not wearing collars," the man added.

Dr Roth laid her hand on my head. "I imagine that this dog," she said, looking into my eyes, "has led a pretty hard life." She stroked my ears. "We'll try to find out if she has owners but, I'll bet she's been on her own for quite a while." She ran her hands up and down my back, then my belly. "Lots of scars. She's been in a few scrapes. And she hasn't been spayed, but that's no surprise."

"What's wrong with her?" asked the boy then. "Why isn't she moving?"

"I'm not sure yet," replied Dr Roth. "She doesn't look too bad. We'll take some X-rays and find out what's going on." She stroked my ears again.

Dr Roth and the woman in blue laid a blanket over Moon, then slid me onto a moving table. They wheeled me out of the room. I never saw Moon again.

Later, after Dr Roth and the people at the vet had finished looking at me and looking at the pictures they took of me, I was laid in a large cage on a bed of soft blankets. At one side of the cage were a dish of water and a dish of food.

Around me were other cages with other dogs in them. One dog was whining and one was barking, but the others were mostly quiet.

I crawled to the dish of food, ate some of it, then curled up on my side on the blankets. I had a pain in my shoulder, the same shoulder that had been injured when George threw me out of the car, and that is the part of my body that Dr Roth had taken the most pictures of.

I had almost fallen asleep again when the man and woman and girl and boy came into the room, followed by Dr Roth.

"Here's our girl," said the vet, leading them to my cage. "She's resting now." The girl and the boy peered in at me.

"What did you find out?" the man asked Dr Roth.

"A few things. I think she's about two years old. She weighs forty pounds, which is a good weight for her size, and she's fairly healthy, although as I thought, she's led a tough life. She's been in a few fights, and I can see an old fracture on her right shoulder, which healed up pretty well on its own. Also, she has fleas and quite a bit of tartar on her teeth. Her main problem, though, is a broken leg. It's badly broken, too."

"Can you fix it?" asked the girl.

"Yes. But she'll need surgery."

"Surgery," repeated the man. "That sounds...expensive."

Dr Roth hesitated. "Well," she said, "there's nothing else seriously wrong with her. If her leg heals, she'll be just fine." She reached into my cage and patted me. Dr Roth had very gentle hands, even when she was touching the most painful parts of my body. "She's such a nice dog," she went on. "She has an awfully sweet temper, especially for a stray. I think she'll make a wonderful pet if we can find someone who wants to adopt her. Speaking of which, as long as she's here, I'd like to spay her and give her all her shots."

"I hate to ask this," said the man, "but who's going to pay for this? After all, she's not our dog."

"I can donate my time," Dr Roth replied, "and I know of an organization that may be able to cover the rest of the cost. I'll call them this afternoon."

"All right," said the man. He was edging towards the door. "Come on," he said, and the woman and the girl and boy joined him. He was about to leave when he turned back to Dr Roth and said, "Thank you so much. We really appreciate what you're doing."

"It's my pleasure." Dr Roth gave me a final pat, then quietly closed the door to my cage.

Sometime later – a day or maybe two – Dr Roth repaired my leg and spayed me so that I wouldn't be able to have a litter of puppies. I don't remember when any of this happened, only that eventually I woke up in my cage feeling very groggy and with a huge pain in my leg. I whimpered and the woman in the blue outfit, whose name was Rachael, called for Dr Roth, who gave me a shot and I fell asleep again. The next time I woke up I felt a little better, and soon Dr Roth was coaxing me out of my cage and encouraging me to walk across the room. This wasn't easy. I was wearing a huge plastic collar around my neck and there was some sort of heavy contraption on my leg, but I couldn't see what it was.

"Good girl! Good girl!" Rachael and Dr Roth said as I hobbled and slid across the linoleum floor. They patted me and gave me treats and told me I was brave and beautiful.

One day the woman and the girl and the boy came to visit. By now I knew their names: Mrs Becker and Margery and Donald.

"The kids wanted to see how the dog was doing," said Mrs Becker. "I was hoping it would be all right to visit her."

Margery and Donald peered at me through the bars of my cage.

"She looks much better!" exclaimed Margery.

"Why is she wearing that thing around her neck?" asked Donald.

"To keep her from biting at her stitches," replied Rachael. "We want her leg to heal as fast as possible. Her tummy, too. She's doing just fine. Here – I'll let her out of the cage and you can see her walk."

Rachael opened my cage and I stepped out onto the floor and scrabbled across it. Then I walked back to Rachael and she wrapped her arms around me and I rested my head on her shoulder. "See how sweet she is?" said Rachael.

"Have you found a home for her?" asked Mrs Becker.

Rachael shook her head. "Not yet. And no one has contacted us about a missing dog."

"Mommy, could we have her?" cried Donald. "Please?"

"Puh-*lease*?" asked Margery.

"Oh, kids. I don't know. We'll have to discuss this with your father."

* * *

The Beckers left and for the next few days I continued to practise walking. Soon my belly was feeling better, the contraption was removed from my leg, and then the collar was removed, too, and a different kind of collar – narrow and colourful – was fastened around my neck. Rachael began attaching a leash to the collar and taking me for walks outside. I didn't like the collar or the leash at first, but Rachael was patient and talked softly to me about the importance of good doggie manners, and after a while I was barely aware of the collar.

One day Dr Roth entered the room, opened my cage, rubbed my ears, and said to me, "Good news, girl! You have a home. The Beckers want to take you."

A few days later, when I was walking almost as well as before the accident and I didn't need any more medicine, Mrs Becker and Margery and Donald returned. Donald was carrying a blue leash and jumping up and down, shouting, "She's our dog now! She's our dog now!" And Margery was grinning and holding a stuffed animal in one hand and a treat in the other.

Rachael clipped the blue leash to my collar and said to me, "We're certainly going to miss you, girl. You were one of our best patients ever. I'm glad you have a home, though." She walked out to the Beckers' car and helped me into the back seat. Then she patted my head and said, "Goodbye," and I could tell she was crying a little.

In the car, Margery sat in the front seat with her mother, and Donald sat in the back with me. As we drove along, Donald said, "You're so lucky. You're going to be our new dog. Your name will be Daisy. We already decided. Remember the dog we had last summer, Mommy? Sasha was a good dog."

"Sasha wasn't our last-summer dog," said Margery.

"Last summer's was Shadow. Sasha was two summers ago."

"Oh, yeah," said Donald. "You're right."

We drove on to my new home.

Summer Dog

My new home was in a large room off the Beckers' house, which I learned was called a garage. I shared the garage with the truck that had hit Moon and me, a car and lots of things that reminded me of my old home at the Merrions' – gardening tools, buckets, ropes, some mice and three families of barn swallows. The barn swallow parents had built their muddy nests in the eaves and each pair was raising four babies. They were all very noisy.

I didn't know much about being someone's pet and living in a home, but I had peeked in enough windows in Claremont and the other towns Moon and I had passed through to know that a lot of pet dogs live inside the main house with the humans. However, I had also seen plenty of dogs living outside in yards, and anyway, the garage wasn't bad.

On the day the Beckers brought me home from the vet, Margery and Donald helped me out of the car, and Mrs Becker said, "Now, Daisy, this is going to be your bed." She pointed to a puffy round cushion in a corner of the garage near an open window. The cushion was dusty and covered with a layer of black and white hairs. "And here's your water and food." She pointed to two dishes near the bed. One was filled with water. The other was filled with something I investigated immediately and found to be pieces of chicken, bits of bacon and some scrambled eggs and toast. "See?" Mrs Becker went on. "You're a lucky stray. None of that dog food for you. You get our table scraps."

I cleaned the bowl in a flash, even though I had eaten breakfast at the vet's.

Margery took me by the collar and led me to my bed. "This is all yours," she said. "And here – this is your very own sheep." She set the stuffed animal next to the bed. "Why don't you lie down now and take a nap?"

"No! Let her come inside. I want to show her my room," said Donald.

"Absolutely not," replied Mrs Becker. "You know the rule, Donald. No pets inside. Daisy is an outdoor dog. Why don't you play with her in the yard? Put the leash on her so she won't run away."

That day Donald and Margery attached the leash to my collar just like Rachael used to do, and they walked me around their yard, which was big, but not as big as the Merrions'. I could see other houses not far away. The yard was pleasant, with trees and gardens and insects, and small rodents hiding in the gardens. We walked until I began to limp on my newly healed leg.

"Oh, she's tired," said Margery. "Let's put Daisy to bed."

Donald and Margery returned me to the garage, carefully pulling the big door down behind us. Then Margery led me onto my bed before unclipping the leash. "There," she said. "You rest now."

I was left alone in the garage, but I didn't mind. I was tired, so I did rest on the bed, even though it smelled of other dogs. At the end of the day Mrs Becker filled my food dish with more scraps, which I ate quickly. Later, when darkness had fallen, Margery and Donald sang me a song that they said was supposed to help me go to sleep.

For a while, each day at the Beckers' house passed in much the same way as the one before. In the morning, Mrs Becker would fill my food dish with scraps. Later, Margery and Donald would play in the yard with me. They stopped clipping the leash to my collar after Mrs Becker said she guessed I knew where my home was now. Margery and Donald threw toys for me to chase after and we tumbled in the grass. When they grew tired of playing, they would lead me back to the garage. At the end of the day, Mrs Becker would fill my food dish again, and more often than not, Margery and Donald would come to the garage to say goodnight to me when it was their bedtime.

Then one day Mrs Becker brought me my breakfast as usual, but Margery and Donald didn't stop to play. They ran through the garage calling, "Bye, Daisy. We're going swimming today. See you later!" I didn't see them until the next day, although Mrs Becker did bring me my supper. After that, sometimes Margery and Donald came to the garage to play with me, and sometimes they didn't. But I didn't mind much when they forgot. The Beckers had stopped closing me into the garage during the day, and I had discovered that I was free to roam around outside. The scents and sounds of the summertime called to me, and I spent my days in the grass and gardens with the bees and bugs and rodents. Then when the afternoon shadows grew long I would return to the garage for supper. This was almost like living at the Merrions' – when Bone and I would roam the woods all day and return to our shed for the night.

Sometimes on the days when Donald and Margery forgot to play with me I would creep up the steps at the front of their house and stand at the door, trying to see through the screen. "Hi, Daisy!" the Beckers would call out if they noticed me. But they didn't open the door.

Until now I had thought pet dogs were never lonely. I was wrong.

Late one afternoon I was sitting in the woods behind the Beckers' house when I noticed something. I was chilly. The days were still long, but they were cooler than before. I noticed this most in the mornings when the garage felt damp, and in the evenings when I would turn around and around on my bed before curling into a tight ball in order to stay as warm as possible. When I had first arrived at the Beckers' the nights in the garage had sometimes been hot and stuffy, even with the window open, but not any more.

I sat on my haunches in the woods, listening for the sounds of animals, of predators, listening to the wind in the leaves and the calling of the birds. I looked above me and saw that one branch of a maple had turned a brilliant colour that I think may have been red, although red is another colour I can't distinguish. And an ash tree was already starting to lose its yellow leaves. Autumn was coming. It wasn't here yet, but it was on its way.

I stood up, yawned, and stretched with my rump in the air. Then I sauntered back to the garage for supper. I waited and waited, but no one brought food. Mr Becker, who had been out for the day, returned in his car, parked it in the garage, patted me on the head without looking at me, and said, "Hi there, Sasha," as he went into the house.

I sat on my bed and waited. No food.

I sat at the garage door and waited. No food.

I walked around to the front of the house and looked through the screen door. No one noticed me.

I walked back to the garage and found that the door

had been pulled down. Maybe later someone would see that I wasn't on my bed. But I don't think that happened because no one called for me.

That night I sat by the garage door until the lights in the house went out. Then I lay down under a rhododendron bush and slept in the garden.

The next morning Mrs Becker raised the garage door and found me sitting on the driveway.

"Oh, my goodness! Daisy, I forgot all about you. I'll bring you your breakfast in just a minute."

And she did. But she forgot to feed me again that evening, so I caught a squirrel for dinner and spent the night on a lawn chair.

After that, the Beckers forgot my food more often than they remembered it, and I was glad of my hunting skills. When my dish was left empty, I scoured the woods. Water was no problem because I could drink from the neighbour's birdbath and also from a swimming pool I had discovered, but I had to be careful because the people who owned the pool would shoo me away if they saw me.

One morning I awoke on the lawn chair, had a drink from the birdbath, then trotted to the Beckers' garage to check my dishes. The garage was open. The dishes were empty, but I barely noticed. There was a lot of activity, and I paused to watch. The car and the truck stood in the driveway, all their doors open. Piled on the floor of the garage were boxes and cases and heavy-looking bags. Mr and Mrs Becker were trying to fit all of the boxes and cases and bags into the car and the truck. They were huffing and groaning and not talking much.

But Margery and Donald were talking a lot, and they didn't sound happy.

"I can't believe summer is over," said Margery. She kicked at a box.

"I can't believe we have to go back to school," said Donald.

"No more swimming, no more rides in the boat."

"Back to the stinky old city."

"Kids, will you please give us a hand?" said Mrs Becker. "Margery, are your suitcases in the garage?"

"They're here. Everything is packed." Margery kicked at the box again.

"Oh, look," said Donald. "There's Sasha. I mean, Daisy. Hey, she's not wearing her collar. What happened to her collar?"

"You took it off her last week, remember?" said Margery. "Where did you put it?"

"Kids, *please,*" said Mrs Becker. "A little help here."

Margery and Donald each lifted a carton. They carried the cartons to the truck.

I trotted to the woods to hunt for my breakfast.

When I returned to the Beckers' later that morning, the car and the truck were gone and the garage door was closed. The door remained closed all day. I checked the other door, the one at the front with the screen, and found that it was closed, too. In the evening, I looked for the lawn chair and discovered that it was no longer on the Beckers' terrace. The yard behind the house had been cleared of chairs and bicycles and toys. Even the big cooking machine and the pots with the flowers in them were gone.

I slept under the rhododendron again.

The next day I saw no sign of the Beckers. There was no sign of them the day after that or the day after that or the day after that or the day after that.

I decided to move on.

Farm Dog

I was alone again. When I set out from the Beckers' house that autumn, there was no Bone to follow and no Moon to walk with. There was no summer family, no Rachael, no Dr Roth. But I knew I could take care of myself.

I wandered through woods and fields and along highways and around the outskirts of towns. The moon grew fat, grew small, grew fat, grew small. The crickets' voices died, and fallen leaves carpeted my path. The wind became blustery and the air frosty, but no snow fell, and I was able to find food.

One day when weak sunlight was filtering through the

bare branches of a small forest, I smelled something familiar, something that made my hackles rise. I growled softly and stalked to the edge of the woods where I saw a group of dogs, as lean as the ones at the resting place on the highway, and just as desperate.

They were fighting one another over an old carcass, leathery now, with no meat left on it. But they fought as if it was a fresh kill. One dog held it between his front paws and gnawed at it. When another dog ran at him, he yipped and snapped, jerking the carcass away, but dropping it as he did so. A third dog swooped in and trapped the carcass between her jaws, but the first dog bit her on the neck and she let the carcass fall.

I slipped back into the forest and crept away. It was time to find a place where I could stay for the winter.

I spent two nights sleeping behind the Olive Free Library. On the morning after the first night a man saw me and set out dishes of water and dry dog food and tried to coax me inside, but I was wary. I ate the food the next night when the library was dark and the parking lot was empty. In the morning I set out again.

I came to a little house in the woods where a man and

a woman lived with their cats. I could see the cats looking out the windows of the house. They didn't go outside, but the woman left dishes of water and scraps on the porch. "TG has been hanging around again," I heard her tell the man. "I saw him twice yesterday." I didn't know who TG was, and I never found out. I hoped he didn't mind sharing his food with me.

I spent one night at the Bearsville Garage, the night of the first snow flurries of the winter. There I found good garbage and a dry doorway.

I spent another night behind a big house on a hill with three sheds in the backyard. In front of one of the sheds lots of logs were stacked. I slept in a niche between the logs and the shed wall. I wasn't warm, but I was dry.

Early the next morning I made my way along the edge of the yard and into some woods. I had my eye on two fat grey squirrels that were chattering and scolding each other. The larger squirrel was chasing the smaller one around and around the trunk of a maple tree. They were paying no attention to me.

I was standing motionless a little distance from the tree, one paw raised, ready to dash forwards, pounce and surprise the squirrels, when *BAM!* I heard a noise so loud it seemed to jolt my body. The squirrels fled up the tree, jumped to the branches of another tree, and disappeared.

I started to run, but since I didn't know where the noise had come from I wasn't sure which direction to take.

Then I heard voices, the voices of men.

"Did you hit it?"

"I don't know. I guess not. I don't see anything."

"But it was right there."

Two men stepped out of the trees. They were wearing dark clothes, and each was carrying a long stick that looked like the polished branch of a tree.

I remembered the man with the gun, the one who had killed Mine when I was a puppy, and I took off running.

"There it goes!"

"That isn't a deer, it's a dog. I think. Anyway, it isn't a deer."

I ran fast, as fast as Moon and I had run to escape the dogs at the resting place. I had gone only a short distance when I came to a large doe lying bleeding on the floor of the woods. Her eyes were open – she wasn't dead – and she turned her head slowly to look at me with glazed eyes. One leg was twitching. I slowed down, then sped up when I heard the men's voices again. I had almost reached the edge of the woods when another blast thundered through the trees.

BAM.

I burst out of the woods.

And I found myself looking down a hill at a small farm. Next to a pond stood a white house with blue shutters. Not far away were two sturdy barns and a fenced-in pasture.

I walked cautiously down the hill towards the pasture. Usually I tried to stay out of sight, but I was in a hurry to escape the men in the woods, and I didn't see anyone on the farm. When I reached the pasture, I jumped easily over the stone wall that bordered it and made my way to the larger of the barns. I paused at the door to listen. From inside I heard little rustlings and cooings, the noises of small rodents and birds, but nothing else. I peeked around the corner. The light inside was dim and the dank air smelled of hay and manure and grain. Across from me were several stalls. Two were empty. A horse stood in the third. He stamped his foot and snorted when he saw me. Maybe he wasn't used to dogs.

I left the barn and investigated the pasture again. I came upon a pile of old vegetables and coffee grinds and eggshells. It wasn't exactly like the Merrions' garbage heap, but it was all right. I learned later that it was called a compost heap. I walked a bit further, warily, my eyes on the barns, the house, the woods.

Far off, on a small rise, stood two cows. I returned to the barn and stood in the door, studying the white house. I saw a truck parked nearby. I saw that the porch was decorated with pumpkins and wreaths of dried flowers like the ones in Claremont before Christmastime. But I didn't see any people.

I peered into the smaller barn. The inside looked very much like the Beckers' garage. A car was parked there, and hanging on the walls were tools and ropes and baskets. At one end was a high wooden bench with more tools laid out on it. This was not a good place to make my home, but the larger barn might be.

"Hal!" I heard a woman call then.

I jumped. Then I turned around and zipped back to the other barn.

"Hal, telephone!"

"Coming!"

Neither of the voices sounded close by, so I peeked outside. I saw a woman, a woman who was older than

Mrs Becker, standing at the front door of the house. A man who looked about the same age as the woman was making his way slowly along a walk to the door. He was dressed in jeans and a flannel shirt, and he was carrying a bucket.

This was Hal, I learned, and the woman was named Jean, and they had lived on this small farm for many years. They were quiet, kind people who took good care of their animals – the horse, the cows, four cats and some geese who had made their home by the pond.

I made my home there, too, but I didn't show myself to Hal and Jean, even though I stayed on their farm during all the days of the cold weather. I stayed while the pumpkins and flower wreaths were taken in and ribbons and evergreen wreaths were put up in their place. I stayed through the snows, one storm so bad that Hal and Jean couldn't leave their farm for three days, but they fed their animals and I dined on grain and mice until I could reach the compost heap again. I stayed while the snow melted. I stayed until I could smell spring in the air, and then I left.

I spent the warm weather wandering, as I had wandered after I left the Beckers' house. When the cold weather arrived, I looked for another farm. And that became the pattern of my life. Farms in the winter, wandering the rest of the time. I had lived on four farms including the Andersons', and another spring had arrived, when I came upon familiar odours, odours that sent me searching for Bone.

The Scent of Bone

Springtime, and I was on the move. I had learned that humans generally make preparations for moves or trips. The Beckers had made preparations for leaving their house, but back then I hadn't recognized the signs. Now I knew what they were: boxes and packing and plans. But I never made preparations for moving on. When it was time to go, I left. It was as simple as that.

And so I had left the most recent of the farms – a large one with horses and stables and people coming and going every day and lots of good hiding places for a dog. One morning I woke up, searched for my breakfast, and spent the day as usual. The next morning I woke up and trotted away.

I was in an area called Lindenfield. I knew that from listening to people on the farm. As I loped along on that first day of travelling, I thought I smelled scents that were familiar. I couldn't quite identify them, though. They didn't say Chipmunk to me or Squirrel or Male Dog or Bread the way some scents did. Still...something about them made me quicken my pace and keep my nose to the ground, snuffling, as I hurried along.

After a while I let the scents tell me where to go. And because I was following the scents, I found myself in areas that were busier than I liked. I walked along a road with cars and trucks whizzing by in both directions. I came to a gas station. (I ran off when I heard a boy call out, "Hey, look at that dog!") I managed to cross a road, waiting first by the side until I didn't think any cars were going to speed into me. On the other side of the road I found myself in a large parking lot where the familiar smells were stronger than ever.

Snuffle, snuffle. I could barely lift my nose from the ground. But when I did, I saw an expanse of cars, and a line of buildings with people coming and going, and some lamp posts, and then a lamp post on a bit of grass with a tree nearby.

This could be only one place.

It was the parking lot were Bone and I had been thrown away. I was sure of it. Odours don't lie.

I was excited. I sniffed all over the lot, not caring if anyone saw me. I smelled food and I ate the end of a hot-dog bun and then some old sausage, but those weren't the smells that interested me. I was smelling *time,* a time long ago when my brother and I were young. And I was smelling *place,* the last place in which I had seen my brother. I didn't smell Bone – I hadn't caught his scent – but that didn't matter. This was the closest I had felt to him since we had been separated.

I sniffed around to the other side of the buildings, to the place where I had found the garbage cans. I sniffed my way back to the tree, and then to the spot where I thought George had stopped the car and tossed us out. Still no scent of Bone, but the other familiar odours kept my nose going and my tail wagging. And they sent me searching for my brother.

On that day, just as I had done on the day I had been

separated from Bone, I hung around the parking lot. I wasn't as small as I had been then, and I didn't want to be noticed, but I was smarter about staying out of sight and about not attracting attention to myself. I waited until darkness was falling, until the parking lot had cleared of people and cars, and then I stood at the edge of the busy road and watched the cars with their lit-up eyes and listened for the *WHOOSHING*. When the whooshing stopped, I ran across the road, ran back to my old woods. And here were the smells of my first winter alone. I nosed around, but I spent only one night in the woods. There was no scent of Bone, so no need to stay. In the morning I set out.

Although I had spent the last few summers roaming woods and fields and keeping to the edges of towns, now I carefully investigated places with human dwellings. I found streets like the side streets in Claremont, but longer and with more houses on them. During the day I watched these houses from hiding places. At night, I inspected them more closely.

No Bone.

I found a long street that reminded me of the one Marcy and George lived on, but I didn't think it was theirs.

It was lined with houses, and I could tell that lots of dogs lived on this street. There were signs of dogs – leashes and bowls and toys in the yards, excrement, too, in some places – and scents of dogs. And I saw several dogs on runs or peeking over fences.

But no Bone.

I wandered on and found another neighbourhood. I nosed into garages. I sniffed up and down the streets at night. I even sniffed around doorways and porches if the houses were dark.

No Bone.

I began to search houses that were further out in the country, in the woods and hills. I explored sheds and porches. I investigated country stores. I searched while the moon changed and the days lengthened, then began to shorten. I searched until I felt a chill in the air. Some of the odours were still familiar now, but not as strongly so as the ones I had smelled at the beginning of the summer. I wasn't sure where I was any more, didn't know how far I had walked. And I hadn't found Bone.

So I moved on. It was time to find another farm for the winter. And that is exactly what I did.

* * *

Winter came and went. Spring arrived, then another winter, then another spring, another winter, another spring, and finally another winter, and I had become an old dog.

I was an old dog with black fur beginning to turn white, a filmy eye, bad hearing in one ear, and very achy bones in the shoulder and leg I had broken when I was young. I was weak, too, and when this newest winter arrived it was the coldest and stormiest one I could remember.

Part Four

Old Woman

Cold.

The cold came early that winter, that winter when I knew with certainty that I was an old dog. No early snow, though. Not like the winter Moon and I had spent in Claremont. But there was plenty of cold. And there were storms that flung sleet and ice out of the clouds, stinging my skin and eyes. I was living at the edge of a town then, my instincts telling me it was time to find a farm for the winter, my old bones protesting at the prospect of the journey. The first of the ice storms came one frigid night, causing school to be closed the next day, which was

Halloween. I had learned that children generally enjoy an unexpected day off from school, but the ones I saw in their yards on Halloween morning were not happy.

"No trick-or-treating tonight," I heard the parents say. "It's icy, too dangerous to go out."

I had spent the night in the shelter of an upended wheelbarrow in someone's backyard. I was dry, but I was so cold I was shaking, and I hadn't eaten since the morning before. Still, I stayed in my shelter until the next day, when the air warmed and the ice started to melt. I waited until the people who lived in the house with the wheelbarrow had left. Then I walked out of their neighbourhood and into some woods.

I travelled for two days and two nights. My limbs felt heavy; they no longer moved with ease. Some days they were stiff, most days they were just plain slow. I was almost always hungry and thirsty; sometimes I was so hungry that I couldn't even feel the hunger pangs. Hunting had become difficult because my reflexes weren't what they used to be. I wasn't fast enough to catch most animals, unless they were unsuspecting. I needed to rely on garbage.

But garbage was easier to find in towns, and I had not forgotten the animal control officers.

One morning I woke up in the grey dawn, shivering in a hollow under an outcropping of rock. I noticed that my hind foot was bleeding. I licked it, then rose unsteadily and set off walking again. I wasn't sure when I had last eaten, only that I needed to find a farm soon.

But I walked all day and saw no farms. I was in the country, and I saw an isolated house here and there, but not a single farm. I fell asleep that night dreaming of Jean and Hal, of the horse and cows and cats and geese, of the warm barn and the compost heap. When I awoke the next morning, stiff and freezing and famished and thirsty, I set out again. I didn't bother to stick to the woods. I was too tired. I walked down a country road. When a car or a truck rumbled by, I stepped out of the way, but I didn't hide.

I travelled this way for two more days, eating an already dead squirrel I found in the road and drinking bad-tasting ditch water. And then the first snow fell.

It began late in the afternoon, just before the winter darkness seeped in. I stopped walking and flopped down on my haunches, out of breath and shivering. I looked around. Only one house was nearby. A long drive led from the road to the side of the house, and a path led from the drive to the front porch. The house was white with black shutters. The yard was tidy. Lights glowed in two of the windows, and good scents came to my nose. I smelled food, and I smelled smoke, which I realized I could see curling out of the chimney.

I turned and walked up the drive, leaving bloody footprints behind me in the snow. When I reached the house I looked behind it and saw a tool shed. I checked the shed and found the door open. I nosed my way inside.

The shed was my shelter for the night. The air inside was cold but dry, and when I peered outside the next morning, I saw that the snow had stopped falling. I tiptoed out of the shed and around to the front of the house. I was sitting underneath a yew bush when a woman stepped onto the porch. She was old. I know the human signs of old age: her hair was white, her face was wrinkled, and she moved as slowly and stiffly as I did. But her face looked kind, and she smiled as she tossed some birdseed onto the ground, glanced at the brightening sky, then slipped inside again.

As soon as the door had closed, I made my way to the seed. I was eating it – in great big gulps – when I heard the door open again. I ran around to the side of the house. And I heard the woman say, "Oh, my. A dog."

I hid in the shed until the afternoon, then returned to the birdseed. Not much was left, but I snuffled up what I could find. I was still snuffling and searching through the snow when the door creaked open. I raised my head. And the old woman poked her own head around the door.

"Good afternoon, dog," she said.

I ran back to the shed. Behind me I could hear the woman calling, "Where are you going? Are you hungry?"

I was hungry. I thought maybe I had never been hungrier in all my life. And so that evening, as I lay in the shed long after the dark had come, I paid attention when I heard a noise from the back of the woman's house. It sounded like a door opening and closing. I peeked out of the shed. The lights in the house were winking off, and soon the house was bathed only in moonlight. I crept to the stoop by the back door. And there before me were two bowls. One was full of water, the other was full of chicken and gravy and mashed potatoes. I slurped up the food, licked the bowl clean, and drank half the water before returning to the shed.

The next morning I was peeping out of the shed when the back door opened. I froze in place and watched the stoop. The old woman stepped outside and peered at the dishes.

"My, she was hungry," she said. "Not a crumb left."

She carried the dishes inside. A few moments later she set them out again. I waited a bit before venturing to the stoop. The water dish had been refilled, and the food dish now contained turkey, cheese and rice. I gobbled up the food, drank some of the water, and hurried to the shed.

That night I found more food in the dish, and the next morning, too. On the day after that, the woman put food in the dishes in the afternoon as well as in the morning and the evening. On the day after *that*, I arose early and waited in the shed for breakfast. Sure enough, as I watched, the door opened and the woman stepped outside, gathered up the empty dishes, and soon returned with full ones, which she left on the stoop, closing the door after her.

I was chomping on a piece of steak when the door opened a crack and there was the woman, standing in the doorway. I stiffened, then backed up.

And the woman said, "Oh, now. For heaven's sake, dog, you must be as old as I am. Why don't you come inside and warm up?"

But I ran off , leaving several mouthfuls of good steak behind. And I skipped lunch, waiting for darkness before I ate again. I didn't want to skip breakfast the next day, though (there had been more steak for dinner), and while I was eating the bowl of scrambled eggs and bacon that I found waiting for me – as I stood on a stranger's stoop in broad daylight – there came the turn of the knob, the click of the door.

I backed away from the food. "Come on, old dog," the woman said. "Enough of this silliness."

I retreated in the direction of the shed.

"You know," the woman continued, "the last thing I need is a dog, but I really think you ought to come inside. You must be freezing."

I put my tail between my legs and kept walking.

"That shed isn't very warm," called the woman. "Not warm at all. If you come inside, you can sit by the fire."

But I couldn't do it. I could not go into her house. Not until the morning when the air was so bitterly cold that I couldn't feel the bottoms of my paws. On that morning, I shivered as I ate the chicken that had been set out. The woman came to the door and watched me. I didn't run away, just stood over the bowl, shaking and trying to swallow.

"Old dog, for goodness' sake, you are a mess. I can see your ribs, you're shivering, and your feet are bleeding. You look like you can barely stand up. Please come inside." She held the door open for me.

I raised my head. I could feel the warmth from her house. I could smell the woodsmoke, and hamburger, good food smells. I looked back at the bowl, down at my feet, my frozen feet. I thought of Marcy and George, of the shouting and swatting and the night in the box. I thought of the Beckers and my dusty bed in the garage. But then I thought of Matthias and Dr Roth and Rachael.

I stepped through the doorway and into the old woman's house.

Addie

The woman led me through a narrow hallway and into a big bright room with a fire burning behind a grate.

"Now you sit there, dog, and warm yourself. I'm going to get some blankets for you."

The woman pushed my rump down until I was sitting before the fire. I looked around the room at the couch and chairs, at a low table with a bowl of flowers resting in the middle, at the framed pictures on the walls. The colours in the room were soft, the fire was warm, the room felt safe.

I heaved a sigh.

"I heard that, dog," said the woman as she returned

with an armload of blankets. "You deserve to let out a sigh like that, a great big sigh. I can tell that you've seen a lot and done a lot, and now you're very tired."

The woman arranged the blankets in a sort of nest next to me. "Okay," she said. "Now you rest here."

She patted the blankets, and I stepped onto them.

The woman sat down heavily in an armchair. "Oof," she said. "My knees don't work the way they used to. I'm not much good at stooping any more." She paused. "Well, dog," she continued, "I suppose I ought to introduce myself. My name is Susan. Susan McGrath. I expect you have a dog name of your own, but I don't know what it is, so I'm going to call you Addie. Unless it turns out that you're a boy, in which case I'll have to think of a different name. But I've been watching you for days now, and I have a feeling you're a girl – and Addie seems to suit you.

"Today, since you're not feeling well, I'm going to put your food and water dishes right here by the fire. When you're feeling better, you can eat in the kitchen with me."

Susan rose slowly and walked out of the room, talking to herself. "I'll have to call the vet," I could hear her say. "Make an appointment for Addie. Goodness, it must be three years since I last called that office. I wonder if Skip is still there."

Susan's voice faded away. I stretched my front legs in front of me and rested my chin on them. I closed my eyes, feeling the warmth from the fire curl over me like a nest of leaves. I didn't open my eyes again until Susan returned carrying the water bowl and the dish of chicken that had been outside on the stoop. She placed them next to me.

"Here you go, Addie," she said. "Breakfast in bed."

I took a drink of water and finished the chicken.

Susan watched me from her chair, then pulled a footstool to the hearth and sat beside me. "Do you mind if I pat you, Addie?" she asked. "I don't want to frighten you." Susan held her hand towards my snout.

I sniffed her fingers. Then I gave them a small lick.

"Ah. You're a kisser," said Susan. "That's fine." She scratched me under my chin, then ran her hand slowly along my back. "Good girl," she said. "Good girl."

I rested by the fire for a long time that day. I was too tired to feel nervous or afraid. Besides, Susan was as kind and as gentle as Rachael and Dr Roth had been. Every now and then she would stir the fire or add another log to it.

When she did she spoke softly to me. "Sorry to disturb you, Addie, but I want to keep the fire going. I want you to stay warm."

Susan was a busy person. I kept my eye on her when I wasn't sleeping. She fixed herself lunch, which she ate in her chair in the living room, feeding me bites from time to time. "I don't usually eat in here," she told me, "but today is special."

After lunch she sat at a desk and wrote with a pen and opened up envelopes and sealed up other envelopes and sorted through a stack of papers, saying, "Junk, junk, junk. Oh, this is important, I'd better keep it. More junk, keep, send to Betsy, junk." And then suddenly she exclaimed, "My goodness, I forgot all about calling the vet." She reached for the telephone. "Hello," she said a moment later, "this is Susan McGrath. I haven't called here in a while." She paused, listening. "Yes, that's right. Yes… Well, I seem to have found a stray dog, an old stray dog. Or she found me. Anyway, I think Dr Thompson should look at her pretty soon. She probably just needs good food and a home, but I want to make sure she isn't sick… Tomorrow? That would be fine. Okay, we'll see you then."

Susan hung up the phone and turned to me. "You're going to have a big day tomorrow, Addie. I have errands to run, and you can come with me. I think we'll go to the pet store. There's a good new one in town. And then, well, I'm not going to lie to you – when we have finished our errands, we'll be off to the vet's. You'll like Skip, though. That's Dr Thompson. My last dog did. Maxie. My old Maxie. Dr Thompson will give you a cookie, Addie."

Susan tidied the papers on her desk and put her pen in a holder. Then she rose, walked through the room and into a hallway, and opened the door to a closet. "Now where is that leash?" I heard her say.

She hauled a bag out of the closet and pawed through it, then put it back. She hauled out another bag, and said, "Ah. Here we go."

I raised my head and watched Susan remove several items from the bag – a collar that looked like the one I had worn when I was Daisy and lived in the Beckers' garage, a leash, a rubber ball and a cloth toy in the shape of a cat. Susan brought the things back to me, laid the ball and the cat on the blankets, and said, "May I fasten this collar around you, Addie? I wonder if you've ever worn one of these. You'll have to get used to it."

I felt Susan's hands clip the collar around my neck. Then she attached the leash to the collar. "I imagine you must have to go to the toilet by now," she said. "I know you don't want to leave the fire, but we have to get you outside for a few minutes. Just a *few* minutes, I promise." Susan tugged at the leash and I got to my feet. I let her lead me outdoors.

We walked around her house until I relieved myself near the yew bush by the front door. As soon as I was finished Susan exclaimed, "Oh, *good* girl, Addie! *Good* girl." And she gave me a biscuit. "We're off to a great start."

Later that afternoon, as I rested by the fire again, and Susan sat nearby in her armchair, the phone rang.

"Hello?" said Susan. There was a short pause before she went on. "Oh. Hello, Mrs Oliver." I glanced at Susan. Her face had changed. It didn't look as soft as it had before the phone rang. "Well, I'm just fine. Thank you for asking… Yes, I know it's chilly today, very chilly… No, I can't think of a thing you can get me. I'm going to go into town tomorrow… Safe to drive? Of course it's safe to drive. All the roads have been ploughed. I've been driving myself for sixty-six years now – since before you were born…" There was a very long pause during which Susan straightened the cushions on the couch, wiped some crumbs off a table, and made a face at the phone. Then suddenly she cried, "Sell this place! Absolutely not. I can manage just fine." A moment later, she added, "I am not snippy," and then, "Oh! There's the doorbell. I have to go. Bye."

The doorbell had not rung. Susan hung up the phone and walked into the kitchen, grumbling, "Who on earth does Mrs Oliver think she is? Half my age and she calls me 'dear'. And since when is my business hers?"

I could hear Susan making banging noises in the kitchen, and thought of Marcy and George. But when Susan returned to her armchair, she was carrying a cup of tea and smiling a little, and she said softly, "I'm sorry I lost my temper, Addie. That woman makes me so mad. But it doesn't have anything to do with you." She patted my back.

And then we sat together in the quiet house, and I watched snow start to fall on the other side of the windows.

That evening, Susan fixed turkey and peas for supper and we ate together by the fire again. But then Susan let the fire die out.

"It's not safe to leave it burning during the night," she said to me as the flames flickered and grew smaller. "But I want you to be warm, so I'm going to move your bed into the kitchen. You can sleep in front of the radiator, all right?"

And that is exactly what I did. After Susan clipped the leash on me and took me outside one more time, she led me into the kitchen and I lay down on my nest of blankets. The snow had stopped falling, but the outside air had been damp and cold, frosty enough to see our breath. I lay gratefully by the radiator.

Susan turned off the light in the kitchen, then in the living room, and called to me, "Goodnight, Addie. Sleep well. I'll see you in the morning."

And I slept warmly all that winter night.

Companions

I slept soundly that first night at Susan's, on my bed by the radiator. I woke up several times, uncertain where I was, but when I looked around and saw the kitchen, saw the water bowl by my bed, smelled the smells of Susan's house, I remembered the events of the day, and I fell asleep again.

Early the next morning, before the sun was up, I heard Susan's voice as she made her way down the stairs. "Addie! Good morning, Addie!" she called softly. She shuffled into the kitchen wearing a long robe, scuffy slippers on her feet.

I lifted my head. Then I sat up.

"Ah. I see you're feeling better. That's fine," said Susan. She bent to stroke me. She ran her hand down my back, then reached under my chin. "Every dog should start her day with a chin scratch," she announced. She moved her hand to the top of my head. "May I pat you here?" she asked. "On your head? Not all dogs like that, I know."

I sat very still. Then I closed my eyes.

"Squinty eyes!" exclaimed Susan. "A wonderful sign."

She picked up my water bowl and emptied it into the sink, then refilled it.

"Hmm, now what should we have for breakfast today?" she said a moment later as she peered into the refrigerator. "I think perhaps I'll have scrambled eggs, and you can have the hamburger and rice that's left over from the other night."

And that is just what we did have, except that Susan also gave me some of her scrambled eggs. It was the first time I had ever eaten them warm, right out of a frying pan. Warm scrambled eggs were awfully good.

"All right," said Susan when we had finished our breakfast, "I hope you're ready for your big day, Addie."

Our big day didn't start right away. First Susan went upstairs for a long time. When she returned, she was wearing different clothes, and she smelled different.

"All gussied up," she said to me. "I'm eighty-two years old, but I can gussy up with the best of them. There's not a thing about me that's old, except my bones."

Susan clipped the leash to me then, and walked me around outside again until I relieved myself. "*Good* girl!" she exclaimed and handed me a cookie.

After that it was time to get into the car. Susan carried my nest of blankets from the kitchen into the garage. "Come on, Addie," she called, and I followed her, even though I was not clipped to the leash.

Susan opened the front door of her car. "Now my Maxie liked to sit up in the front seat, right next to me," she said. She turned and regarded me. "I don't know if you've ever ridden in a car before. I hope you won't be scared. Maxie loved it. You can look out the window. Sometimes you see cats or squirrels or other dogs. It really can be very entertaining. Maxie used to sit up tall and stare straight ahead. I called him my co-pilot." Susan had arranged the blankets on the seat of the car. She looked down at me. "Are you ready, Addie? This is your big adventure."

I sat by the car and looked back at Susan.

Susan patted the seat. "Jump on up here, Addie."

I scrambled onto the blankets.

"Good girl," said Susan, sounding relieved. She shut the door and then walked around to the other side of the car and eased herself behind the steering wheel. Soon we were driving down the lane.

I watched the country fly by outside the window. At first it looked familiar. I smelled familiar smells, too. I saw snow, lots of snow, some trees, and here and there a house. Eventually the houses appeared closer together, and the smells became unfamiliar. Then we reached the edge of a town, a town that was bigger than Claremont, but that reminded me of it anyway, and I sat up taller.

Susan glanced at me. "This is the nearest town, Addie," she said as she parked the car on the street. "It's called Hampton. This is where I do all my shopping and errands. Are you ready for our errands? I really do have quite a few. Our first stop is the dry cleaner's. Now you sit here and I'll be right back. If you get bored, you can chew on this." Susan handed me an enormous object that looked like a bone but didn't smell like any bone I'd ever found in the woods. I licked it, then I placed it between my front paws and set to work chewing on it.

Susan left me alone for a few minutes. When she returned she was carrying an armload of things in flapping plastic bags, which she put in the back of the car. We set off again.

"Next stop, the post office," said Susan. "Goodness, it's nice to have a companion along. How's that bone, Addie?"

I chomped away. I wasn't even looking out the window any more.

Susan drove to the post office next, where she went inside with a small package and came out with a stack of envelopes. Then she took us to a place called a bank, to a place called a pharmacy, and finally to a bakery.

After the bakery, when we were sitting in the car that now smelled of butter and sugar and bread, Susan said, "Well, Addie, the next stop is going to be your big treat today. I suppose I should really give you the treat *after* we go to the vet's, as a reward, but I'd have to drive us way out of the way in order to do that. So you'll get the treat first.

"Listen to me, talking a blue streak! I haven't spoken so much in months. But this is silly – I'm going on and on as if you could understand every word I'm saying." Susan rested her arms on the steering wheel and looked thoughtful. "Well, maybe you can," she went on. "Who knows? Anyway…off to Pet Town."

Susan pulled out of the bakery parking lot and drove us back through Hampton. A few minutes later she said, "Here we are! This is Pet Town, Addie. It's brand-new. You can buy anything you need for your pet here. *And* people are allowed to bring their pets inside. So come on in with me, and we'll find what you need."

Susan clipped the leash to my collar, and we walked inside a huge building. When we stepped through the doors, my nose was met with so many smells that I raised my head, sniffing, and then stood on my hind legs to get the best smells possible.

Susan laughed. "There's a lot of good stuff in here, isn't there?"

I had never experienced anything like it. I had sniffed around The Wagging Tail in Claremont, and other pet stores, but I had never been inside one. Now I saw shelf after shelf of things, many of which were unfamiliar to me, but that smelled very, very interesting. Later, after I had been to Pet Town several more times, I learned what these things were: supplies for cats and other animals (which Susan and I ignored), dog food (in cans and in bags), dog toys, dog beds, dog chews and dog clothes. The clothes looked like the outfits I had seen children wearing at Halloween, and I was relieved when Susan said she thought dog clothes were silly and we could walk right by them.

"Now, let's see," said Susan, "you'll need a proper bed, not those old blankets. They'll be all right for the car, but not for your bed. And we have to get some food. I know eggs and hamburger and scraps are tasty, but you need a balanced diet. Here's the food Maxie used to eat. Oh, I must remember to ask Skip about vitamins." Susan turned a corner and we walked down another aisle. "My! Look at all these toys, Addie…"

Susan had found a shopping cart and she pushed it along, filling it with things she took from the shelves. She consulted a list that she pulled out of her purse. "Hmm. Bed, check. Food, check. Stuffed toy, check. Chewies, check. Throw toys – I don't know if you'll be up for chasing toys, maybe I'll just buy one."

When Susan was finished shopping she had bought so many things that someone had to help her carry them to the car.

"And now," she said as we drove away, "it's off to the vet's." She looked at her watch. "We'll be right on time."

The moment Susan led me inside Dr Thompson's office I recalled the smells from my stay at Dr Roth's. And I remembered my visit there. I remembered Moon lying so still beside me, but I also remembered Dr Roth's gentle hands, and Rachael, and I didn't feel nervous as we settled ourselves in the waiting room. I sat at Susan's feet and from time to time I glanced over my shoulder at her. When I did, she would smile and pat my back and tell me I was a good girl.

The waiting room was warm and I was tired, so I was beginning to fall asleep when a young woman stepped into the room and said, "Mrs McGrath?"

"Yes," said Susan, and she stood up. "Sorry to wake you, Addie, but it's our turn."

In the little examining room I was lifted onto a metal table, where I sat until a man came in carrying a clipboard, and said, "Susan. It's wonderful to see you again. Who do we have here?"

"Hi, Skip," said Susan. "This dog has been hanging around my house for a long time, and yesterday I finally persuaded her to come inside. She's lovely, but I don't know anything about her. I thought I'd better have her checked out."

Dr Thompson began examining me. He was very gentle, like Dr Roth. He looked in my mouth, he ran his hands down my back and over my belly, he listened to my heart, and he looked carefully at my paws. "Well," he said, after a long time, "this dog isn't in bad shape, considering she's a stray. Are you sure she's a stray?"

"Positive," replied Susan.

"Because she's been spayed. I can see the old scar on her belly. She must have been someone's dog once."

"I'll bet she has a lot of stories to tell," said Susan.

Dr Thompson looked down at me. "She seems a bit weak and dehydrated, and she's on the thin side. I see evidence of ear mites and fleas — not out of control, though – and I notice that her feet have been bleeding. I think she has some cracks in her pads. I should probably check for worms and parasites. Her vital signs are good." Dr Thompson paused. "I'd say this dog is nine or ten years old."

"Nine or ten," repeated Susan. "In dog years that's almost sixty."

"She'll need shots, too, of course," Dr Thompson went on. "And she could stand a good bath. Do you want us to go ahead and do everything? Give her injections and get the medicine for the mites and so forth?"

"Absolutely."

"It won't be cheap."

"I know."

"Does that mean you want to keep her?"

"Want to keep her? Why, she's mine already," said Susan.

That night I fell asleep by the radiator in my new bed, a teddy bear at my side.

Two Old Ladies

The winter days at Susan's passed slowly and gently, like leaves falling from trees. Every morning I awoke in the kitchen in my bed by the radiator. I always woke before Susan came downstairs, and I would roll over and lie on my teddy until I heard Susan's footsteps. When Susan entered the kitchen she would greet me with pats and kisses and chin scratches, and then she would make our breakfast – dog food for me, and toast and eggs and fruit for her. She always gave me a bite of warm eggs, though.

In the mornings I kept Susan company while she was busy at her desk or with her sewing or puttering around the house. Sometimes she talked on the telephone.

Sometimes one of her friends would drop by and Susan would fix tea. Susan made sure to walk me around outside the house every so often, and each time I relieved myself outdoors she gave me a cookie. During the first few days I was at Susan's I relieved myself indoors a couple of times, and Susan would show me those spots and say, "No cookie, Addie." Then she would clean the spots with something in a white bottle, and eventually I understood that I was not to relieve myself indoors. I also understood that Susan would make sure I went outdoors often enough so that I wasn't uncomfortable.

At lunchtime, Susan ate a small meal in the kitchen. I did not get a meal at lunch any more, although Susan usually gave me a bite of hers. In the afternoon, Susan and I would climb in the car and run errands together. My favourite places to visit were Pet Town and the bakery. Susan always brought me into Pet Town with her, and sometimes someone in there would give me a treat.

In the evening, Susan and I ate dinner in the kitchen. Afterwards, Susan usually worked at her sewing or read a book. We would sit together on the couch. If possible, I would rest my head in Susan's lap.

I had been living at Susan's for a while – I wasn't sure exactly how long, because I was less aware of the shape of the moon than I had been when I lived outside – when the doorbell rang one morning, and Susan exclaimed, "Goodness, now who could that be? I'm not expecting anybody."

Susan had been sorting through some cartons that she had brought into the living room from another part of the house. She left them on the floor, and called, "Who is it?" as she hurried to the front door.

"It's Mrs Oliver," I heard someone reply.

I watched Susan. She stopped walking, stood very still in the hallway, closed her eyes for a few seconds, and muttered, "Oh, *drat*." Then she opened the door.

"Hello, Mrs Oliver," said Susan.

"Hello, dear." A stout woman stepped into the hallway, tracking snow in after her.

"Would you like to take off your boots?" Susan asked, looking at the wet marks on the carpet.

"Oh! Oh, yes, of course. It's still *so* chilly out there," said Mrs Oliver, as she stooped down to slip off her boots. "I don't know how you're managing out here all by yourself in this cold."

Susan looked perplexed. "I have a furnace," she said.

Mrs Oliver's face coloured. "I meant with the shovelling and driving and all."

"Mac is still coming by to shovel me out, just like always," said Susan. "And they do seem to plough the roads so quickly nowadays. I never have to wait long before I can get out."

Mrs Oliver had removed her coat. She hung it in the closet in the hall. Then she stepped into the living room. "Why, Susan, I see you're getting ready for Christmas. That's lovely. How did you get all these boxes in here?"

"I *carried* them," said Susan. "I can still —"

"My heavens! What on earth is that?" Mrs Oliver interrupted her. She was pointing at me.

"It's a dog."

"Well, I know it's a dog, dear. I meant, what is it doing here?"

"Her name is Addie and this is her home."

"Oh. Susan." Mrs Oliver looked deeply disappointed, as if Susan had chewed up a couch cushion. "Now how are you going to manage a dog? Where did she come from anyway?"

"She'd been hanging around the house. She was nearly

frozen to death. But I've been taking her to Skip, and she has a clean bill of health."

Mrs Oliver didn't seem to be listening. She had bent down and was running her hand through the carpet.

"What —" Susan began to say.

"I'm just checking for flea dirt."

"Flea dirt. Tsk." Susan looked disgusted. "Addie does not have fleas." She paused. "She does not have ear mites, either. Or the mange. She's in perfect health. She's just old."

"And so are you," replied Mrs Oliver, standing up. "Really, my dear. How *are* you going to take care of this dog? She's too large for you to pick up. And she's decrepit. Is she even house-trained?"

"Of course she's house-trained."

Mrs Oliver sniffed. "Well, I'll admit that the house smells fine." Susan stared at her. After a moment, Mrs Oliver turned away from Susan and approached me. I was curled up on the couch. "She seems a nice enough dog," Mrs Oliver said finally. "But really, Susan, have you thought this through? An old dog is only going to get harder to care for. What are you going to do if she can't walk? Or if she becomes incontinent? If you ask me, you should take her to the shelter and let them find a home for her with younger people."

Susan drew herself up straight. "Mrs Oliver," she began, "Addie is good company—"

"I'm sure that's true."

"And furthermore…" Susan hesitated. "Furthermore … Oh, my. It's starting to snow. You should probably be on your way. Before the roads get too slippery."

Mrs Oliver glanced outside. "All right. But, dear, I suggest you think about what I said."

Susan planted herself in front of Mrs Oliver and said firmly, "I will do no such thing. Addie is here to stay." Then she crossed through the hallway and held the door open while Mrs Oliver slipped into her coat and boots again and stepped onto the porch.

"Have a good—" Mrs Oliver said, but Susan had already closed the door. She turned to look at me. "Hateful woman," she exclaimed, and I thought she said it rather loudly. She returned to the living room and sat next to me on the couch. "Did you understand any of that, Addie?" she asked, stroking my muzzle. "I hope not. But if you did, I just want to assure you that I have no intention of taking you to a shelter. You're mine, and I'm yours, and this is our home."

* * *

That night Susan put me to bed in the kitchen as usual, and for a while I lay by the radiator and gazed outside. The moon must have been full because Susan's yard was lit up, and I could see the new snow coating the tree branches. Suddenly, without knowing I was going to do so, I stood stiffly and walked to the bottom of the staircase. I looked up. The first floor seemed far away, and I wasn't used to stairs, although I had climbed Susan's once or twice. I let out a sigh before I began to make my way up the steps. I knew where Susan's bedroom was, and when I reached it I nosed through the partially open door, then stood on my hind legs and peered into the bed.

Susan stirred, but she didn't seem surprised to see me. "Hello, old lady," she said. "What are you doing up here? You should be in your own bed."

I stared at Susan for a few more seconds, then dropped to all fours and attempted to jump onto the bed. It was very high, though, and I slipped back to the floor.

"Oh, dear," said Susan. She was as stiff as I was, and she moved slowly as she pushed back the covers, hung her legs over the side of the bed, and finally stood beside me. "Come on back downstairs."

I didn't move.

Susan smiled. "Oh, all right," she said. She shoved a footstool next to me. "Here, use this." She coaxed me onto the stool and placed my front paws on the bed. I jumped, and Susan shoved my rump up, and the next thing I knew I was crawling under the covers and Susan was climbing in beside me. We slept together all night.

And that is how we have spent every night since then.

Home

It is another summer. Susan and I have lived together now for many changes of the moon. Every morning and evening we eat in the kitchen. At night we sleep in Susan's bed. During the day we keep each other company, and now that the warm weather is here, we take short walks near Susan's house. Recently Susan whispered to me, "Remember when I said the last thing I needed was a dog? Well, that wasn't true, of course. I do need you, and I'm glad you're here."

We're sitting side by side on the couch when she says this, and I slide into Susan's lap and heave a huge sigh.

Many years ago, I thought my life would be whole if I could just find Bone again. But I didn't find him. And Mother was gone, and Moon was gone, and I had decided I was complete on my own. Then I found Susan. I didn't think I needed a human any more than Susan thought she needed a dog. It turned out that there was room in my heart for a human after all.

The long-ago days – the days of Mother and Bone and the shed – have become fuzzy and have blended with images of Moon, of my travels, of other people and houses, of hiding places; a tangle of memories leading to Susan. I burrow into her side and listen to her heartbeat. With my eyes closed, I might be in the straw-filled wheelbarrow again, nestled against Mother, listening to the first heartbeat I knew. I open my eyes and tilt my head back to look at Susan's lined face. She smiles at me, and we sit pressed into each other, two old ladies.

Q&A with Ann M. Martin

How did you decide to write a story from a dog's point of view? I love animals and have wanted to write an animal story for a long time. My dog, Sadie, was born to a stray dog who had been seen wandering along a highway, almost ready to give birth to a litter of puppies. Magnolia, Sadie's mother, was rescued, and she and her puppies were lucky, because they all found good homes, but I've often wondered what would have happened to Sadie if she had been born in the wild, what her life would have been like. I decided that if I was going to tell a dog's life story, only the dog herself would know the entire story, so I wrote from her point of view. It was a fun challenge. Often while I was working on the book I would observe Sadie and wonder what was going on in her head.

Was there anything particularly challenging about writing Squirrel's story? Actually, writing from a dog's point of view gave me certain liberties. For instance, in order for Squirrel to tell her own story, she had to have acquired language, so I had the fun of imagining how that might have happened. On the other hand, dogs can't communicate, at least not the way Squirrel does, but I wanted her story to be believable; she still had to be a realistic dog. I did some research on dog anatomy and behaviour, and of course I was able to observe Sadie, but even so, I made mistakes. For example, about a third of the way through *A Dog's Life* I remembered that dogs are partially colour blind, so I had to go back to the beginning of the story and take out all the references to colours that Squirrel wouldn't be able to see. Details like that took me by surprise more than once.

Along Squirrel's journey, there are people who aren't very kind to her. Do you think these people

intended to be cruel, or did they just not know any better? Both. There are characters in the book who intentionally harm Squirrel and other animals; for instance, the kids who throw rocks at the dogs. And there are people who are guilty of neglect but who probably have no idea they're doing anything wrong. The people who adopt Squirrel as their "summer dog" fall into this category. Sadly, in reality this happens frequently. People get a puppy or a kitten in the spring when it's little and cute. But by the autumn, the animal is larger and perhaps no longer so cute, and people's lives become busier. So they abandon their pet, or turn it loose, thinking it can fend for itself, and that's just not true. If you adopt a pet, you're responsible for it for the rest of its life.

Have you ever rescued a stray dog? No, although Sadie's mother was a stray, and I'd heard the story of Magnolia's rescue. But I've worked with stray cats and have fostered several hundred over the years, so I've known plenty of abandoned and abused kitties. And one of my cats, Willy, was rescued when he was about five months old after he and another cat were tossed out the window of a car speeding down a country highway. (That's where I got the idea for the chapter about Bone and Squirrel being thrown out of the car at the mall.) A friend of mine found Willy in a parking lot, fed him, and brought him to my house. At the time I had two cats and wasn't thinking about getting another, but I couldn't *not* take him!

What advice can you give to aspiring writers who want to write a story from an animal's point of view but maybe don't know where to begin? I think it's important to focus first on the story you want to tell, and not necessarily on the fact that you'll be writing from an animal's point of view. In other words, do you want to write an adventure story? Or a fantasy in which the animals have special powers or can talk? Remember, too, that the animal can tell its own story, as Squirrel did (in her own words), or a narrator can tell the animal's story, so think about whether you want to write in the first person or the third person. This should help you figure out where to begin!

Acknowledgements

A number of years ago, I began working with a local animal rescue organization. Since then, I've become acquainted with many wonderful people in my community, and I would like to acknowledge them and the selfless work they do every day.

Among these people are Susan Roth, Helen Mendoza, Linda Takacs, and everyone associated with A.W.A.N., the Animal Welfare and Adoption Network; Dr Orman "Skip" Leighton and the loving and dedicated staff at South Peak Veterinary Hospital; and Ann Gregory and all the other people who graciously act as foster caregivers to animals awaiting permanent homes. There are more people, many more – other veterinarians, other caregivers, other people who have started rescue groups, as well as the people at PETsMART who generously donate space in each of their stores as an adoption area for homeless animals. They are all to be commended.

I would like to thank Robin Murphy, Vice President of Companion Animal Placement in Hoboken, New Jersey, for her thoughtful consideration of the manuscript.

And I would like to mention Jean and Hal Anderson, who are the best neighbours anyone could ask for, and who, for eighteen years, gave Tico the rescue donkey the best home he could have asked for.

Finally, I want to thank Laura Ruth Godwin and Sadie Lynn Pupmore for turning me into a dog person.

Also by Ann M. Martin

If you enjoyed Squirrel's adventure, you'll love...

"If you can read, you'll love this book."
THE NEW YORK TIMES

how
to look
for a
lost dog

Author of the internationally
bestselling "Baby-Sitters Club" series
ANN M. MARTIN

OUT NOW!

ISBN: 9781474906470